WALTZ THROUGH ETERNITY

MARGARET TEEGARDEN

Inquiries and Book Orders should be addressed to:

Great Writers Media
Email: info@greatwritersmedia.com
Phone: (302) 918-5570

ISBN: 978-1-960605-87-0 (sc)
ISBN: 978-1-960605-86-3 (ebk)

S it back and relax. Let your mind slip right into the characters of the pages that follow. When you completely drift into the lives of the characters you'll experience frustration, anger, hurt and despair and soon you'll feel pain and agony that lasts for all eternity. This type of suffering can only be relieved by truth and everlasting love. The main characters of the book are Charlotte and John. They were both born and raised in the Richmond area of Virginia. After they were married, the Company John worked for transferred him to the West Coast to work in their Plant out there. They were there for ten years when finally they decided they wanted to move back home and raise their children in their home town. They moved back and moved in with John's parents. They had a house big enough to accommodate the families. But it was to be for only a short time. John went to work immediately and Charlotte had the task of finding the family a house to live in. At first they thought it should be easy, but after some months have passed they still found nothing. Real Estate was either to expensive or ready to fall down.

Charlotte has become terribly depressed. She needs her own home and in her depressed state she needs some time away from John's parents. So she gathers the children and takes them for a drive in the country. She drives to a place where they can stop to look out over the city. The day was beautiful and the children enjoyed playing in the deep grass and weeds. They were having a great time and the day passed very quickly. Charlotte realized the time and collected the blankets and things so they could head for home. They were all in the car and she began to pull out on the road when she felt the urge to go in the opposite direction. She had no idea why, but she followed her instincts. She drove down the road and soon she realized it was almost dark. She had to find a place to turn around and head for home. She looked ahead and saw an opening in the weeds and decided to turn in there and get the car turned around. As she drove into the opening she looked through the windshield and saw the outline of the roof of a very large house. A place that she doesn't remember ever seeing before. She quickly turned the car and headed for home. But the whole way home she had a nagging feeling to go back to the old house and didn't have the slightest idea why. The feeling was overwhelming. She was being drawn to the old place and didn't understand why. She's never seen the place before in her life. But soon everything begins to unfold. The house was the wedding gift for a young bride to be from her fiance.

He was so happy that she excepted his proposal that he promised her the biggest and finest house in all the lands and so it was. Soon the wedding plans began and the construction of the house was also underway. Everything was going beautifully and the plans fell into place just like clock work. But then as the construction was nearing a close there came a terrible set back. The Civil War broke out and the young man being an Honor student from a fine Military Academy was called upon for duty. At that point in time the young couple was devastated, but they had to look forward and pray for his safe return. Soon it was time for the young man to go off to war. As they were saying their farewells, the young man had his loving Sarah make him a promise. His request was that no one was to live in the house until his return and then they could live in the house forever together. Sarah kept her promise to Joe, but he never returned. He lost his life mysteriously to the war. After Sarah received word that Joe was dead she vanished. Both their lives were taken maliciously and the truth laid hidden for over a Century. But their souls wander aimlessly at the place they both loved so much. Now over a hundred and thirty years later, Charlotte's destination is to free the restless spirits. But it could cost her dearly. She could lose her own life in the process if anything went wrong. Sarah's spirit is very mild mannered at first but then she becomes violent. She's extremely angry, she wants desperately to be with the Captain. Her longing is uncontrollable and she wants peace at last. Through Charlotte she finally has the chance to free both hers and the Captain's spirits. The truth must be found and Charlotte is the only one who can find it. She is the key and soon with the use of her physical form the truth is found. But still the spirits won't rest. There is still an evil force to prevent eternal rest for the lost souls.

Chapter One

Driving down the highway headed east. Charlotte looked into the rear view mirror. She saw that both the children were sleeping. She smiled and thought how beautiful they are. She looked over at her husband and for a second, watched him as he slept. It's been a long trip and everyone is exhausted and just a few hours more they'll be back home in Richmond, Virginia. They were all glad to be going home.

Shortly after John and Charlotte were married, the company John worked for transferred him to the west coast. They wanted him to start a new company and get it pretty well underway. They failed to tell him that it would take ten years to get it operating the way they wanted it to. Every time John mentioned going back home they used some lame excuse on why they needed him there. But finally John said, either you send me home to work in the company back there, or I quit. Luckily the company agreed to send him home and even helped to pay the expenses for them to move back. Which made things a lot easier for the couple.

Charlotte pulls the car off the highway. There was a small diner right up ahead and the family hadn't eaten their supper yet. Charlotte parked the car and woke everyone up. The children were tired and grumpy and Charlotte told them it was time to eat. That made them happy, they said they were starving. John on the other hand only wanted coffee and to go to the restroom to wash up a little bit. But when he got to the table, he decided to join the family in a meal. While they were eating John and Charlotte discussed the rest of their trip. They decided to drive straight through until they got to John's parents house. So they all finished their meal and got back on the road, as soon as possible.

It's about two A.M. and the scenery started to look real familiar to John and Charlotte. They were both born and raised in the Richmond area and their families go back many generations there. They both missed home very much and was glad to be finally going back. Both their children were born on the West Coast and never saw Richmond. Both the families have visited at one time or another, but even so it's been two years or so since they've seen the children.

John and Charlotte felt bad about that, but really couldn't do anything. They simply couldn't afford to go home. No matter how bad, they wanted to. Nothing else seemed to matter now. John just turned the car into the driveway of his parents house. Everything was dark, John's parents were in bed. They didn't expect them until sometime the next day.

But with John and Charlotte both driving, they made good time. Charlotte said, what are we going to do, they're in bed. John said, in total excitement, we wake them up. We haven't seen them in a long time, they won't care. So John and Charlotte woke up the children and went to the door. They rang the doorbell several times before John's sleepy father came to answer it. When he saw who was standing at the door, he yelled, mother come see who's here. John's mother came down the hall to the stairs. She bent over the railing and looked down. She couldn't believe her eyes. She ran down the steps to greet them and smother the children with kisses. She turned to John and told him that they should have called, and she would have fixed them something to eat. John said, Hush mom and give me a hug, you have plenty of time from now on, to fix us something to eat. Because from here on, we're going to be right here at home. We've decided on the way home that we were never, leaving

Richmond again. After all the hugs and hello's were out of the way, they all got settled in and got ready for bed. There was a lot of work to be done the next day. When morning came, John's mother was up early and fixed a hearty breakfast for the family. After awhile, no one woke up and she couldn't stand it anymore.

She had to see them and talk to them. She smiled to herself and said, I know how to get them up. She went to the living room and turned on the stereo as loud as it would go. She remembered doing that very same thing when John was home and it was always very effective. And still is, because it wasn't long until the family started coming down the steps one by one. When John came dragging himself down the steps. His mother chuckled and said, still works "huh"? John still rubbing sleep from his eyes, smiled and say's, yes, it sure does. The children ask if something was wrong with the stereo. They thought it must be broken. All the adults laughed and said, no it's not broken, come to the kitchen and get your breakfast and I'll explain, said their Grandmother. They all went to the kitchen and as promised, John's mother told the children that when their dad was a young man, she used to do that to him when he didn't want to get out of bed. The children didn't find it as amusing as the adults but excepted it and ate their breakfast. While the adults discussed their trip and the plans for the day.

First things first, John started by cleaning out the garage. That was the only place they had to store their furniture until they found a house to buy. Meanwhile Charlotte was calling all the local Realtor's to see what properties they had for sale in the vicinity. The couple had to be very selective and find one within their means. Which really shouldn't be to hard, all they want is a place to call home.

Even if it needed a lot of work. They didn't want anything elaborate, just a fixer upper will do. So Charlotte started gathering information on places for her and John to start looking at. But to their surprise, it was a very difficult task. They looked for weeks and found nothing to their liking. When they found something they would be interested in they couldn't afford it. John had to work late one day and Charlotte was feeling a little depressed, she decided to take the children for a drive in the country. Just to get away from things for awhile. She drove for about two miles just checking out the scenery when she came to a place to pull off the road and look down over the city. Her and the children got out of the car, the weather was beautiful. So they just stayed there and enjoyed the fresh air and the view. The children played hide and go seek in the weeds while Charlotte just sat and enjoyed just being out of the house and away from all the Realtor's. But being out and enjoying her self, time flew by. Before she knew it, the sun was going down. She told the children it's time to head home.

They all got in the car and Charlotte got back on the road to head home, when she felt a sudden urge to turn around and go the other way. So, she did and she didn't know why. She drove a few more miles down the road and thought she had better find a place to turn the car around. It's getting dark and she doesn't want to be out to far or be to late with the children. So, she thought she would turn into the next place she found. As she drives down the road, Charlotte see's a lane that turns to the right. She swings the car into the lane, she stopped the car and started to back out when she looked up, and down the lane, was the silhouette of a large house. She thought, that's strange, I never noticed that place before and I've lived here all of my life. She turned the car and headed back to town. All the way home she had the strangest feeling that she had left something behind. So, as soon as she arrived at the house, she checked to be sure she had all the blankets and things, that they had out of the car. She thought, that's really weird, why do I have this feeling. Everything's here, but Charlotte's still puzzled by the way she feels. So, she simply puts it aside, and gets the children into the house. When they opened the door to go in John was waiting for them. He said hello to the children and kissed Charlotte. He asked, where have you been? Charlotte explained, that she took the children for a drive in the country. John said great, how did it go? She told him, that the view is still as beautiful as ever, then proceeded to tell him about the old house they saw. He asked, what old house? I don't remember seeing a house out there. Charlotte said, that's strange I didn't either. She then got the children ready for bed and tucked them in for the night. Charlotte went down stairs to join John and his parents in the living room.

They were all watching the news and talking about the things they missed, while living on the West Coast. Just making up for lost time. When John asked Charlotte a question, she was in another world. John said, honey is something wrong? Charlotte said I don't think so. I just have a feeling, that I left something out by the road today. But I checked and everything was there. Silly isn't it. John smiled and said to her, maybe you'll find out what it was tomorrow.

Everyone said their good nights and headed for bed. John was exhausted, and went right to sleep. While Charlotte lay there watching the shadows dancing on the walls, from the trees and lights outside. She couldn't sleep. That feeling came over her again, even more powerful than before. It was a long night for her, when the alarm went off for John at daybreak, she was still wide awake. Charlotte got out of bed and went down to make coffee for John. When he came down, Charlotte was fixing breakfast. John said to her, Honey you really look tired. Did you get any sleep at all? She said, Not much! That feeling kept haunting me and I can't shake it. John said he had to go and told her to relax. It can't be all that bad. He kissed her and went out the door. Now she thought, it's time to get the children ready for school. After she got the children out the door. Charlotte helped to get the housework done.

She told John's mom, that she was going to ride around and see if she could find some houses for sale by owners. She said, she wouldn't be to late and went out the door. As she pulled out of the driveway, she thought about where she would look first. She decided to go out the same way she did the day before. After driving a short distance she thought, she might as well go back to where she and the children were yesterday. She really needed to find out if she left something there. Shortly she came to the place where they were the day before. She pulled the car off the road and got out, she could see the indent in the grass where they had spread their blankets. She combed the area to see if she could find something, but she found nothing. Charlotte went back to the car and leaned up against the driver's door. She stood there for awhile and looked out and enjoyed the view. She was thinking about houses and how very nice it would be if they had their own place. At that point she knew she had better get moving or she wouldn't get anything accomplished today. Charlotte got back into the car and started the engine. She pulled the car into drive and was ready to pull out when she got that strange feeling again. Only stronger this time and for some reason she couldn't shake it. Suddenly she had the urge to go to the old house that she had seen the day before. She didn't know why but she really had the need to see the old place. It was almost like some unknown force was drawing her to it.

The next thing Charlotte knew is she was at the lane to the old house. She turned in and went just a little ways when she stopped the car. She sat there and looked at the grounds around the house. It was so grown up that you could hardly see the place. She thought, that might be the reason her and John didn't remember seeing the house before. They never saw it because the foliage was so thick. She drove down the lane very carefully. She needed to see more, her curiosity has gotten the best of her. When she got close enough to make out the outline of the house. She decided to get out and walk from there. She certainly didn't need to get stuck in the lane. No one knew she was there and the nearest house was about a mile down the road. Charlotte fought her way through the weeds and briers to get a better look at the house. It was huge, and Charlotte was thinking it must have been very elegant in it's day. It was also very protected, the tree branches wrapped around the house. They looked as though they were embracing the outside of the structure. Protecting it from the elements of time. The windows on the bottom floor were hardly visible to the eye. The shrubs and weeds are grown up to the top of them. The only thing you can see is the frame work at the very top. The front porch has been completely taken over with ivy. The ivy grew up over the entrance way and the windows under the roof on the porch have been covered so heavy that one can't see through to the inside.

It's like the inside of the house is being closed off from the outside world. No one can see out and absolutely no one can see in. The secrets the old place has, are to remain a mystery to the outside world. Charlotte thought that her imagination has gotten the best of her. She would really like to see the inside of the house or just get a closer look but wouldn't dare get any closer. She had no idea what was in the weeds around the place and decided she had better get out of there. She struggled back through the weeds to the car, she got in and started to back down the lane. It was difficult with all the brush, but she managed. She got back on the road and started towards home. She didn't get very far when she got that feeling again. She felt like she was meant to go to the house and the urge came over her to turn and go back. She tried very hard to ignore the feeling and headed for home. But all the way home she had the nagging feeling that she had left something behind. The next few weeks went by very quickly. The Realtor's set up several appointments for John and Charlotte to see houses. But of all the houses they looked at there was none they were really interested in. All the places were either to expensive or needed to much work for the money. So, they decided to keep looking until the right place came along. They both felt sure that something would come along soon. They were the type to think positive and never give up.

The Realtor's were doing the very best they could do. But for Charlotte, that wasn't good enough. She was getting very impatient, she needed her own place. Charlotte looked over the newspaper ads everyday so she would have at least one place a day to look at. But even so she couldn't find anything to her liking. After a few weeks of all the hassle, she got tired of all the running around and just about gave up. John and Charlotte even thought about renting for awhile but that idea fell through and John ask Charlotte to hang on for a little while longer and something was sure to turn up. Charlotte agreed and continued to look for a place that would suit them. At John's parents house things were beginning to get really nerve racking. There simply wasn't enough room. Charlotte was feeling like she was intruding on John's parents and their privacy. John's parents insisted that everything was okay, but Charlotte sensed that they were feeling put out. After all, they have lived alone most all of their lives and now they have a whole house full. And Charlotte knows from experience, how hard it is to give up your home. Even if it is family it's still difficult, so she decided to keep up the search day after exhausting day.

Chapter Two

THE HOUSE

John was getting pretty settled in his job. All the experience he had running the plant on the West Coast sure came in handy back here. It was really tough at first because he now has a boss over him. Where at the other plant, John was the boss and giving orders for John was a lot easier than taking them. But he's finally getting used to the way things are now. He even realized that he doesn't have to take the heat for every small thing that doesn't go right. He even thinks he might like it this way a little better. He also looks forward to the weekends with his family. At the other plant he had to work all the weekends and got off a day or two in the week, if he was lucky. The weekend has come and John and Charlotte planned on spending the days with the children. They decided to take a drive in the country. This way they could kill two birds with one stone. They could have a picnic and look for a house, at the same time. So, bright and early Saturday, they packed a picnic basket and headed for the country. They drove for miles and enjoyed the scenery. They haven't seen the country side for years and was quite pleased to see how things have changed, since they moved away. They came across a couple farms for sale. They were both of a very large scale. John said, he would like to own one of them but was afraid that he wouldn't know the first thing about running one. He told Charlotte he was a city boy and they joked about what he would do if he ever had an encounter with a cow. He wouldn't know which end to milk. They laughed and Charlotte said, but honey you don't milk cows. Your supposed to milk ducks, I think. They were laughing so hard that John had to pull off the road. Ironically it was the same place that Charlotte took the kids for the view of the city. They decided to have their picnic there. The children liked this spot very much. They played hide and seek in the weeds and ran through the woods, they had a good time there. While they played, John and Charlotte laid on the blanket and enjoyed each others company. They talked about all sorts of things and what they used to do when they were younger. Then the conversation came to the subject of the old house. John told her he didn't remember an old house down the road where Charlotte was talking about. Charlotte ask him if they could drive down the road and she would show him. He said sure we don't have anything better to do, so let's go. They gathered their blankets and the picnic basket and headed down the road. They were both excited, they felt like they were going on an adventure. They drove for a mile or so, when on the right side of the road came a small opening in the weeds. Charlotte said to John, turn here. John said, turn where there's no place to turn. She said nonsense, I turned right here when the kids and I were here. There's a road in those weeds. John said, okay, I hope your right. As he made the turn the weeds seemed to open for them.

John could see his way clear to the top of the knoll of the old lane. When they got to the top, they looked down the lane and there stood the old house. Just as Charlotte discribed it. John was totally amazed at what he saw. He looked at Charlotte and said, your right there is a house down there. And then he said, but look at it. No wonder we never saw it. It's completely covered with the trees and weeds. You can't even see the roof. Charlotte said, come on let's get a closer look. We can walk in from here. John was a little reluctant to get any closer. He said this is private property and we're probably trespassing already. Charlotte said, that's nonsense. There doesn't look like there has been anyone around here for years and years. John grinned at Charlotte and the adventurer took over in him. He said, let's go, but we have to be real careful. There are probably a lot of snakes in the brush that we can't see. So each one of them took a child by the hand and led them down the lane. There was weeds and briers everywhere. The Briers clung to them and scratched them until they bled. John tried to fight his way through in front of everyone. He finally gave up, he told Charlotte to stay where she was and he would be right back. He went to the car to see if he had anything in it to cut through some of the brush. The only thing in the trunk was a tire iron. When he came back to where Charlotte and the children were. He said, all he could find was the tire iron and that even if it didn't cut the weeds, it might beat them down enough to make a path.

John passed them and went further down the lane. He was pretty successful at making a path. It was a small path but that was all they needed to get closer to the house, to get a better look. They got almost to the bottom of the lane when they came to an old well. John cleared some of the weeds from around it and said to Charlotte. Look at this, all the stones are in their original position. The only thing wrong with the well is the roof it's a little rotted from the weeds holding moisture on it. The rest of it's beautiful. The stones look like they were just laid there. John beat the weeds around the well, he made a big circle and found two stone benches on each side of the well. He said to Charlotte, look at these. They must have been beautiful in their day. Now John too, is really excited. He wants to get a closer look at the house. So, before Charlotte knew what was happening. John was almost to the house and Charlotte and the children, were right behind him. John was almost to the front porch when all of a sudden, came a chilling wind. It hit them right in the face. John turned to Charlotte and said, what the hell was that? Charlotte laughed and said, what's the matter John, are you afraid of ghosts? John mumbled to himself and went back to beating the path to the porch. Soon he came to a stone walkway. He tried to follow it but didn't know which way to go. It went off in three different directions. One was to the well, the other went to the house and the third led to what John thought was nowhere.

He was curious, he wanted to get to the house first and then find out where the other walk led. He felt sure it led to something, but had no idea what. John finally got to the porch steps. He cleared away some of the ivy from them and couldn't believe his eyes. The wood in the steps looked like new cut wood. It wasn't rotted at all, it wasn't even weathered. John was stunned. He pointed to the steps and told Charlotte to look at them. She was equally stunned. They talked about how was it possible that a place stood for so long and not show any signs of wear. Charlotte walked up the steps to get a closer look at the doorway and the porch. John followed her on to the porch. They pulled some ivy away from the railings and the rails look like new also. They couldn't understand what had happened. The house was completely preserved. Just like the day it was built. All John and Charlotte could figure was the trees and weeds protected and preserved the place from the element of time. Next, they both grabbed the ivy on the side of the house and pulled it away. Just as they expected, the stone was beautiful. But why? They don't understand, what could be the reason for the house to be completely preserved.

John left Charlotte on the porch to see what she could. She continued to pull the moss and ivy from the porch and walls. Meanwhile John has gone to find out where the other path leads to. Charlotte got a place cleared so she could get to the door of the house. She wanted to see the inside, if she could. She wiped some of the dirt from the glass and tried to see in. It was impossible with all the dirt on the inside of the glass, not to mention how dark it was inside. Charlotte was really curious about the house. While the children had their own interests in the bird nest on the porch. Charlotte continued to clear the doorway. She felt all the way around the door frame to see if there was a key or some way to open the door. Charlotte was disappointed when she didn't find a key to fit the old lock. But she did find something of interest. As she rubbed her hands around the frame of the door. She felt something chiseled in the stone, She went back and rubbed the dirt away and tried to read what it said. At first she uncovered numbers. The numbers read 1859 and right above the numbers was the word BUILT. After she read what was written in the stone, she realized that the house was built just before the Civil War broke out. That along with everything else they had discovered fascinated her and she simply had to know more. Charlotte was always a sort of Civil War buff. She was interested in the people and how it affected the lives of all the people who lived through it. She enjoyed reading books and watching movies about it. Anything that had something to do with the War, Charlotte was interested in. She was intrigued by the fact that they fought for a cause so great, that brother would kill brother for what they believed in. Their Country and the love of it.

Charlotte feels like somehow she has taken a part in all of it. When she reads or watches a movie she feels like she knows the grief and misery that was felt at that time. When she reads some of the stories of the young soldiers it touches her heart in a way nothing else ever could. When she would read about a young man dying she would cry uncontrollable and didn't have the slightest idea why. And to watch a movie she always had a box of tissue close at hand. But never the less, she was compelled to read or watch. She was fascinated in that time and era. But why, she never understood. Something inside of her always needed to know more. Charlotte was interrupted in what she was doing, John was yelling for her. He had made his way out the other walkway. Charlotte got the children and went to join him. On the path some distance from the house he found an old family cemetery. The headstones at the entrance of the graveyard read. Father; Aron McMasters. Mother; Lottie Hampton McMasters. The stones had been weathered but John was curious to find out what the dates read and scratched and scrapped until he could read them. They read, 1824 or 34 as the date of Aron's death. The other dates couldn't be read. Back behind the big stone at the entrance was about twenty or more smaller stones. Some of the dates were very clear and some were not readable at all. John and Charlotte walked back through the cemetery, when the little boy yelled for his mom to look.

She looked up at the same time John did and they both saw the shadow of a man standing in the brush at the edge of the woods. They watched and the shadow didn't move, it just slowly disappeared. John thought immediately that there must be some logical explanation for the shadow. He looked up and checked the position of the sun and checked the trees. He told Charlotte the willow tree was the culprit. The tree cast a large shadow. John look up and said, that's got to be the largest willow I've ever seen. John walked under the tree to check out the small headstones under it. He looked back at Charlotte and said come on there's more stones over here. Charlotte walked towards John when all of a sudden she stopped dead in her tracks. John turned to see what was the matter. Her face went chalk white, she was frozen in her tracks and shaking. John ran to her and tried to talk to her but she only stared straight ahead. John looked ahead of her and saw something Hugh in the weeds behind the tree. He too, got a very eerie feeling. The thing looked very spooky, what ever it was. John stood a few minutes and checked it out from a distance. He realized then, that it was a tomb. Right away he wanted to go and check it out. But Charlotte on the other hand, was very reluctant to go near it. John and Charlotte were having the time of their lives, they were like a couple of kids on an adventure. Up until now Charlotte was having the time of her life.

But when she realized there was a tomb there she got very nervous and tense. For some reason she was feeling fear and didn't want to get any closer than she had to. But John convinced her that she was being silly. He reassured her that who ever was in there was surely dead and had been that way for a long time.

So Charlotte agreed to go closer with John and look it over. It's getting late in the day and Charlotte was hoping John would give up for today, but he told her he had to get closer to the tomb. His arms were getting tired from swinging the tire iron. But he kept thrashing away at the weeds. Finally they got close enough to see that there was an inscription on the tomb. It wasn't readable at first, but John pulled the weeds back and wiped the dirt away. He looked at Charlotte and said, come on. You got to see this. Charlotte said, what's so different about that one? I've seen tomb's before. John turned to look at Charlotte and said, this one looks like it was just put here. It's in perfect condition and the stones are beautiful. But that's impossible, the weeds have completely covered it. John was really curious now, but decided to call it a day. The sun was going down and they got the children by the hand and headed for the car. They followed the same path out and by the time they got to the well it was almost dark. John got about five feet from the well and stopped dead in his tracks. He told everyone to be quiet a minute. They all stood and listened. John said, do you here that? Charlotte said yeah, I heard it before.

John said, you heard that music before and didn't say anything to me. She told him she heard it when she was on the porch earlier but you called for me to come out there and I completely forgot about it. John ask her if she could tell where it was coming from. She said, I think it's coming from the house. Isn't it beautiful? John said sarcastically, yeah it's fantastic. It sounds pretty damn weird to me. Lets get out of here. The music for some reason upset John. Charlotte thought maybe it upset him because it was to late for them to find out where it was coming from. So they both dismissed the music and headed to the car to go home. They decided that they would do more exploring there, some other time when they wanted to spend the day together again.

Chapter Three

THE STRANGER

F all is approaching very quickly. The children will be going back to school soon and still they haven't found a place of their own. Charlotte's feeling pretty down about the whole situation. She wants a place of their own so bad, she can hardly bare living in the home of John's parents any longer. Things aren't really bad, but Charlotte is feeling real uncomfortable. She feels like every time she has to do something, she needs to ask permission. She needs her own home to run, although John's family is wonderful to them. They go out of their way to tolerate all the upset a family of four can contribute to a household. They go out of their way for John and his family but they need their privacy too. Charlotte being a woman, understands all that but John on the other hand thinks everything is going well. But of course he doesn't live there all day. He works and comes home to relax and go to bed. So, he really doesn't have to cope with all the confusion. And most definitely does not understand the need for a woman to have her own place. Charlotte, all day while John's at work. Tries to keep herself real busy. She does what she can for John's mother at the house and then goes about her own business. She has the chore of finding her family a home. She still has several appointments a week to see houses and they take her all around the city and out in the country. She of course wants to live in the country but would settle for a nice place on the out skirts of town.

But even so, she still hasn't found anything to her liking. The Realtor's are about to give up on her. Their beginning to believe that there wouldn't be a place in the world to suit Charlotte. But of course their wrong. Charlotte wants a place with a lot of character and charm. She doesn't care if it needs a lot of work. She has a lot of time to work on it, she figures she has the rest of her life to make a house a home. But it's just the matter of finding the right place. John and Charlotte wake to another day. John has to be at the plant extremely early today. Some big shots are coming in from another plant and John's boss ask him to come in early and show them around. Charlotte got John off to work and was reading the morning paper when John's mother came down. She woke up on the wrong side of the bed, she was in a very bad mood. Charlotte ask if there was something wrong and she snapped at her. Charlotte knew right then and there that she had better get out of the house for the day and let her be alone for awhile. So Charlotte woke the children and told them to hurry and she would treat them to breakfast. After we eat we'll go for a drive in the country and maybe if God's willing we'll find a house today. It wasn't long before everyone was ready to go. They decided to eat at a diner on the outskirts of town. They ate their breakfast and discussed where they would go. Jeannie the oldest child suggested that they go to their other gram-ma's house and see her and pappy.

Charlotte said, that's a wonderful idea. We haven't seen them in a few weeks and they'll be delighted to see us. So it was settled. When they got to Charlotte's parents house. They pulled into the driveway. Charlotte looked everything over and remembered living in this very house while she was growing up. She always loved the place and after she moved away she missed it very much. So she always felt real good about going home even if it was, only to visit. She doesn't get to her mom's house as often as she likes but to her mom that doesn't make any difference. She was always excited to see them, no matter how often they came. Charlotte's mom heard the car pull into the driveway. She was at the door with it open, before Charlotte even got the key turned off. The children jumped out of the car so fast, they didn't even take the time to shut the doors. Charlotte smiled and closed them, before she went to the house. She was pleased to see the children so happy to be there. Charlotte hugged her mom and ask, where's dad? Her mom told her that he was on a job. She said, this is the time of year when he doesn't get much time off. He's very busy with everyone trying to get their work done before winter sets in. He even had to hire extra guys to try to get caught up. But even at that rate he wouldn't be caught up until at least Christmas. Charlotte knew what her mom was talking about. When she was growing up he was always busy. He took great pride in his work and was an excellent Contractor.

He built new homes and renovated old ones. And he loved his work, he was never shy about showing anyone his jobs and most of the time that's all he talked about. By this time the children were already in the back yard. They were on the swing talking to the neighbors children. Charlotte mom said, come on we'll get some coffee and go out on the porch to sit, it's a beautiful day. They got the coffee ready and some homemade rolls and headed for the porch. Charlotte was really glad she came over today and she really needed to relax at home. She kicked off her shoes and propped her feet up on the railing. She said to her mom, you know I really love this place. I want a place that makes me feel this way. Why don't you and dad move out and I'll buy this one. Charlotte was joking of course and her mom knew it. They both laughed and her mom said, some day you'll probably get the house but I'm not ready to give it up just yet. If you get my drift and winked at Charlotte. They laughed and joked awhile and just simply enjoyed each others company. Charlotte's mom finally said, honey I wish you could come over more. I realize your busy trying to find a house and all but I and your father would like to see you and the kids more. And I miss you very much, I enjoy having your company. And there are some things you just can't get to much of. Charlotte knows exactly how her mother feels. Because she too, feels the very same way.

The two women sat on the porch for it seemed like hours. They talked about everything that they've missed for the past ten years. They talked about the children and John. His job and how things were going at the plant and even their living on the West Coast.

Finally the conversation came to houses. Charlotte's mom ask if they found anything to their liking. She told her mom no and told her that she wouldn't believe how many places she looked at. But there was always something wrong with them. Either they wanted to much money or they were ready to fall down and they would still want a fortune for them. It's like a rat race trying to find a house suitable for them. So at that point they relaxed and watched the children playing in the yard. The morning passed very quickly. Charlotte and her mom enjoyed the time together very much. They decided to go and work in the garden for awhile and gather some of the vegetables. They discussed the prices at the grocery store and soon the subject came back to houses. Charlotte got quiet for awhile and her mom ask if something was troubling her. She told her mom no there was nothing wrong she was just thinking about a house that her and John went to see lately. We saw it one day when we were going for a drive in the country. Charlotte said, you know mom there's something about that old place. I can't put my finger on it but I can't stop thinking about it. Then she told her mom about the house and about all the things they found when they were there. Her mother listened with deep concern.

She was very anxious to see what Charlotte was talking about. If it's the house that her mom thinks it is, she has her own thoughts about it. Although she was never really a suspicious person. She was beginning to become really unnerved about the conversation. She didn't even know why. Only that she was feeling fear for her daughter for some reason. At this point she ask Charlotte to stay away from the place. It's not safe there. Charlotte chuckled and said, what's the matter mom are you afraid of the boogie man. Her mother got a little angry with Charlotte. She said no, I'm not afraid of ghosts but there are a lot of strange stories come from that old place. And they might not be all wrong. Charlotte laughed and said, mom do you realize how silly you sound. Her mom said, go on and make fun of me if you like. You can laugh all you want but I believe there's something really wrong with that place. It's been empty for over a hundred years. No one has ever lived in the place since it was built. So that in it's self has a story behind it. The whole conversation has become very amusing to Charlotte. Mom I don't know what kind of stories your referring to, but it's all nonsense as far as I'm concern. Ghosts and goblins are in the mind of the people who think about them. Oh, don't get me wrong, I to believe in spirits and the unknown but I surely don't want to conjure up a ghost.

Especially before I even see inside the place. There has to be a logical explanation for all the things the people talk about. There just stories, plain and simple. Her mom said, maybe so but they've been enough to keep people away for all those years. So that tells me, there's something weird about that old house. Charlotte said okay, you win, what exactly are the stories about the place. Her mom said okay, lets go and get comfortable and I'll tell you what I know. "And so the stories goes". Sometime in the mid eighteen hundreds. There was a young man,the son of a very rich and respectable family. He was a very intelligent young man. At a very young age he started his own business, what kind of business, I don't know. But he become very rich at a very young age. He was quite popular around with the young ladies and he was supposed to respect them very much. He never really got serious about any one of them. He grew tired of the run of the mill hum drum every day life and decided to go to Military School. What school he attended, I'm really not sure about. But he did very well there. While he was away, he meet the girl of his dreams and fell madly in love with her. And of course she felt the same way about him. It was like they were meant for each other as soon as their eyes meet. Or what some people say was love at first sight. It's been said, that he loved the girl like no other man could love a woman. He cherished her.

They became engaged to be married. When they announced their engagement, he also announced that he would build her the finest and the biggest house in the territory. Well he kept his promise. Construction started on the house almost immediately. The young man was very enthusiastic. He wanted to be married as soon as the house was finished. They say that the wedding was to be at the house and the reception was to be on the grounds. They planned a hugh wedding and started the plans right away. A couple of months had gone by and things were coming together very well and right on schedule. Then came the blow of their young lives. A tragic change of plans were in order. The Civil War broke out and the young man was called to the Army. The young couple was devastated. The young lady kept her wits about her, even though her heart was breaking. She told her young man not to fret, the love they had would last an eternity if need be. She truly believe it and soon he did too. Believing at this point was all they could do. They tried hard to keep their faith. Even though there young hearts were breaking. Soon, the young man went off to war. But before he left, he had his bride to be make him a promise. She promised that no one would live in the house until he returned from the war. Then they would live there happily together. She convinced the young man that it would be only a short time and the war would end, then they would be together.

The wedding would go as planned and it would be the most glorious wedding in the land. So with that thought in mind, the young man made ready to leave for the war. The girl kept her promise. The house construction continued as planned. After awhile the house was completed and ready to move into on their wedding day. But the war continued for two more years and all they could do was wait it out. They wrote to each other faithfully and continued their undying love for each other. When the house was completed, the girl kept herself occupied by buying the furniture and having made, what they would need to start keeping house. All the rooms were finished as far as furnishings and the linens were put on and made ready to move into without much effort. The girl was working at the house when she received a letter. She could hardly wait to read it, she was always happy to get word from him. The letter was good news. The young man has been promoted to Captain. He is now known as Capt. Joseph Owen McMasters. He was a good Captain, he was very popular with his men and they respected him very much. He was very dedicated to them, he fought right by their sides and didn't expect them to do anything he wouldn't do himself. One day the Captain put in for a couple days leave. He was granted his leave because he wasn't far from his hometown when the request was made. Three days before he was to go on leave. His regiment was ordered into battle.

The Captain was mortally wounded and died shortly after. But he lived long enough to scribble a note to his loved one. It read;

Sarah, My Dearest

My love for you will never die. My body is going to fade but my spirit will be on earth with you until the end of time. I'm sorry I won't be with you in the house. But believe me my dearest when I say, "I'll be with you forever". I'm tiring now, must say Goodbye My Love.

With All My Love
Joe

The final words of the letter were very hard to read. The Captain died as soon as he finished the letter and it was almost scribbled. But Sarah knew what it read.

The Captains parents went to Sarah as soon as the word came of the Captains death. Sarah was at home with her parents when they got the message. Sarah was crushed, she ran out of the house and got in the buggy and went straight to the new house. She spent days there by herself and wouldn't let anyone in. She wanted to be alone in her grief. She wouldn't leave the house. Finally her mother had enough. She was truly worried about Sarah. She went to the house to try to get her to come home. When she got to the house the door was left open and all she found was a note written by her daughters hand. The note read;

Who ever finds this; Tell my family, I love them but I can't go on. I have to be with my loved one and there is only one way. I must join him. Tonight I have a last request. Promise to leave the house just the way we left it. No one is to live in it until we can be together again. That was the promise I made to Joe before he went to war and I want the promise fulfilled. When the time is right and only at that time someone will be able to live in the house. And it will be the spirit of myself and my beloved Joe. Until then, I bid all my loved ones farewell and will walk with you and the Lord when we meet again.

P.S.
Please don't weep for me. I'll be in the arms of the man I love.

Yours truly,
With all my love. Sarah

Charlotte said to her mom, Wow that's quite a story. But mom how is it that you know the story so well? Her mother looked down at the floor and back to Charlotte. She said, the story has been handed down through the generations. At this point Charlotte was very confused. She said, mom what are you saying? Her mom proceeded to tell her that to her knowledge the story is true and that there is a diary to prove it. You see the woman who wrote the diary was the girls mother. And also she was the twin sister of my great great grandmother. Charlotte said, so what your saying is that the girl was your great Aunt. Her mother said yes, and someday when you have some time. We'll go into the attic and dig out the old trunk that's been handed down and I'll show you what's there. Charlotte said, that would be fantastic. I love digging through old things. And at this point, the day has passed quickly and Charlotte had to get back to the house. John would be home soon and she had to help fix supper.

It was about six when she got home. John's mother already had the meal fixed and ready to go on the table. So Charlotte set the table and waited for John to come home. She could hardly wait to tell him about all the things she found out about the old house. She was so keyed up about the story that she wanted to go right back out and explore some more. She felt like it would be okay because the house was to be the house of her great great Aunt. John pulled into the driveway and Charlotte met him at the car. She was so anxious to tell him the story. The second he opened the car door, Charlotte met him and started to ramble on about the old house. He laughed and said, Honey I know you want to talk but can I at least get cleaned up first. He took her by the hand, kissed her and said, Hello dear. Come with me and you can talk while I get cleaned up. While John was in the shower, Charlotte told him the story that her mother told her.

Every once in a while John would peek his head out and ask a question about something he didn't hear or understand. He too, grew more curious about the old place. Charlotte even told John about the letter. John was out of the shower when he turned to Charlotte and ask, what happened to the girl? Did she kill herself or what? Charlotte said, I don't really know. Mom never said and I didn't think to ask either. John told her, well we're just going to have to find out somehow. My curiosity is killing me and I won't be able to deal with the not knowing. If you know what I mean? But never the less, they both had to be patient at least until Charlotte talked to her mother again.

The next morning, Charlotte got John off to work. She fixed the children their breakfast but never got her mind off the old house. That seemed to be the only thing she could think about. She couldn't concentrate on what she was doing. She kept thinking about the girl and what could have possibly happened to her. Charlotte's curiosity got the best of her, so as soon as she got the food on the table she headed for the telephone to call her mom. But her mom had already gone out. The phone rang and rang, Charlotte being disappointed, decided that she would have to find out on her own.

Charlotte ask John's mom to keep an eye on the kids for awhile. She told her that she was going to try to find some information about the old house. John's mom was reluctant to answer her, she felt that Charlotte had no business going out there alone. She finally ask Charlotte, if she would be alright out there by herself. Charlotte was delighted with her concern and said with a smile, yes don't worry I'll be fine. So everything was set and Charlotte got ready to go. But that didn't stop John's mother from worrying about her. It took Charlotte about an hour to get everything done before she left. But soon she was on the road and headed to the old place. The closer she got to the property the more she felt the need to go there. Then she thought this is strange, but somehow I have the feeling that I'm going home. She shrugged the feeling and laughed at the thought.

Charlotte passed the place where they looked out over the city. While she was driving by she thought about the last time she and John were there. How they enjoyed the day together and before she knew it, she was at the lane to the old house. As Charlotte turned the car off the road she got a real eerie feeling. She ask herself, should I go on or should I go home? She decided to go on. She drove in the lane as fast as she dared to. She thought, I don't want to get stuck here. No one would find me until after dark. John would know right where to look for me, but I don't want to be here that long all alone. She drove in the lane carefully. When she got just to the top of the knoll, she stopped, parked the car and sat there staring out the windshield. She couldn't believe how fascinated she was with the old place. She thought, how beautiful it must have been in its time.

It was frightfully huge, but even so it looked like a mansion. It was very difficult to see how big the house really was with the trees hovering over it. There was ivy growing up the sides of the house and into the trees. Then from the trees the ivy hung back down like a curtain. The roof was hidden in all the foliage and at this point Charlotte's imagination was in full swing. She pictured the trees like an umbrella, protecting the house from the elements and preserving it until the Mistress and her Captain came home. She realized though that all that would be fantasy. Since it's been over a hundred years. They'll never come home and it seemed a terrible waste. Charlotte got out of the car and made her way through the weeds. She thought how fast everything had grown. It had only been a short time since John had beaten down the weeds. Now there's hardly a path at all. She continued towards the house and struggled through the briers and weeds. Finally after a dozen of scratches on her arms and legs, she made it to the well. She stopped to rest and wiped the blood from her scratches. Then headed on to the house. After fighting her way to the porch she was in need of a rest. She was exhausted. She sat on the top step of the porch. She looked up to see if she could see her car. When she realized that she couldn't see it she felt a rush of fear. She quickly thought about being by herself and decided she had better leave this place.

When she stood up her heart was pounding. She ran down the steps and back to the well. She stopped to get her breath. When she finally could control her breathing she listened. There it was again. "The Music". How beautiful it is. The music was very old fashioned. Charlotte remembered her grandmother talking about music from the old days. She spoke about Mandolins and harpsichords and Charlotte couldn't help but wonder if that was the sounds she was hearing. She recognized the music, it was definitely a waltz of some kind and it was soft and romantic. She was enchanted by it. Mesmerized she froze where she stood and soon all the fear she felt was gone. She only knew the sound of the music. She slowly turned around and walked back towards the house. She was in a complete daze. She was aware of everything around her, but felt like she had no control over her actions. Something had brought her back to the house and as she got to the porch the music stopped. Charlotte came back to her senses and was trying to figure out what just happened. She began to wonder if her imagination wasn't getting the best of her. Charlotte stood facing the front door of the house. She reached up with her shirt tail and wiped dirt and grime from the stained glass window. She saw her reflection and wasn't content with that, she wanted to see inside. She continued to wipe the window to make a hole big enough to see through. She pressed her face against the window but it was no use. The house was dark inside.

She felt extremely disappointed and stood up to turn and walk away. As she turned her heart took a leap. She saw her reflection in the glass and behind her, looking over her shoulder was an old man. "A Very Old Man". Charlotte felt instant panic and her mind was racing. What will I do? She decided to turn around and confront the man but then she realized that the man in the glass could be from inside the house. She started to turn very slowly. Thinking if he's behind me, how will I get away. She turned half way around and the old man was right behind her. She froze in her tracks, her heart pounding. She was terrified.. The old man spoke to Charlotte. He said, sorry I scared you Missus. I saw your car and reckoned you must be lost. You are aren't you? She couldn't answer, she had to collect herself. She was so scared she almost wet her pants but after a few seconds, Charlotte answered him. She said, No! I'm not lost. I came here out of curiosity. He said, what are you so curious about? Charlotte was reluctant to answer, she really didn't know how to take the man. He sounded like he was protecting the place. Like a caretaker or something. So she was very cautious as she spoke. She told him who she was and why she was there. After she talked awhile she noticed, the man hung onto her every word. When he spoke again he did so in a much softer tone. Charlotte told him that she meant to leave a while ago and got to the well when she heard music. So she came back to the house to see where it was coming from.

The man said, Oh yes! The music, beautiful ain't it? They call it the "Sweethearts Waltz". Charlotte said, yes, it is beautiful, but where does it come from? The man said, don't rightly know, Missus, but it does come from in thar somewheres and at night it's a wee bit eerie round here, plays late in the night sometimes and if your real close to the house you can hear someone crying. The hair raised on Charlotte's neck and she got chills up her spine. She said, so what your saying is that the house is haunted. The man strained to find the right answer. He chose his words carefully and said, No! I really don't think that the house is haunted, but I do know that at times thar is someone in thar. I don't believe in ghosts and he chuckled out load. Charlotte said, if you don't think it's haunted then who's in there and why. Maybe it's the people who own the place and if so, I'd like to talk to them. Charlotte turned back to face the door and pounded on it. She was excited. She thought if someone was in there maybe they could tell her if the house is for sale. As she pounded she got no response. She turned to talk to the old man and he was gone. Charlotte felt really uneasy. The man vanished, he disappeared as fast as he appeared, with not a trace. Charlotte stepped lightly on the old boards of the porch and every step she took the wood creaked. She felt a bit nervous about the whole thing and knew she had to get out of there as quickly as she could.

Charlotte ran down the steps passed the well and headed straight to the car. She didn't stop for a breather this time. She would rest in the car when she got there. Charlotte was almost to the car when she slipped and fell. As she was picking herself up off the ground she saw a shadow move by her. She was scared to death. She wanted to look but couldn't bring herself to, all she wanted to do was get to the car. She pulled herself to her feet when suddenly she heard the music again. This time she ran to the car as fast as her legs would carry her and headed home. As Charlotte was driving, she was thinking about everything that happened at the old place. She wondered if the house was possessed by the supernatural or if the old man was telling her stories to keep her away. She didn't really care one way or the other. All she knew was that she had to find out as much as she could about the place. At home she pulled up to the house and John pulled in behind her. She didn't realize how late it was, but was glad to see him. She couldn't wait to share her experience with him. As soon as they got in the house. Charlotte started to ramble on about what had happened. John was angry at Charlotte for going to the house all alone, but on the other hand, he was fascinated with the story. He and Charlotte decided that they should do some research on the old house to find out what they could. John too, was very interested in the old man. What part did he play in all this and why?

After they discussed everything, Charlotte told John she thought she should go talk to her mom and find out everything she could. And even go in the attic and see what was in the old trunk. The next morning Charlotte made a point to get to her mothers house early. She called her mom to make sure she would be home and agreed to get an early start. The attic was really cluttered and it would take a lot of digging to get to the old trunk. Charlotte pulled in the driveway to her mothers house at 8:00 A.M. They took coffee to the attic with them and got started right away.

Chapter Four

THE DIARY

In the attic Charlotte was fascinated, she had no idea her mother had so many antiques and collectibles up there. They were both like children in a candy store. They didn't know which box to go through first. Around noon they decided to put the heirlooms away for now and find the trunk. They moved boxes after boxes and finally way back in the corner they spotted the old trunk. The walk down memory lane was over for now, it was time for serious business. Charlotte and her mom drug the trunk out of the corner and into the light. They decided to get more coffee and then get started. They made a quick trip to the kitchen and went back right away. They were both very anxious to see what all was in the old trunk. Charlotte's mother hadn't seen the contents of the trunk since she was a young girl. Her mother went through it and put it away and told Charlotte's mom to keep it forever and she promised she would, and now it's time to open it once again. Charlotte was excited, she looked the trunk over and remembered seeing trunks like this one in old movies. It was beautiful, it was dusty and dirty, but beautiful none the less. It was trimmed elegantly the hinges and lock were brass and after all those years it's still in excellent condition. Charlotte's mom made a detour on the way back to the attic.

She stopped in her bedroom to get the key which she kept in her jewelry box. Shortly she came up the steps and said, Wah Lah! here's the key. Now we get down to serious business. Charlotte and her mom sat down on the floor in front of the trunk.

They looked at each other for a minute and her mom slowly put the key in and unlocked the trunk. She opened it and Charlotte gasped as she looked in. Her mom said, are you alright? Charlotte didn't hear her, she just stared into the trunk. Her mother got a little shook up and touched Charlotte's arm. She said, honey are you O.K.? Charlotte said, What mom? What did you say? Her mom said, I ask if you were o.k.? When I opened the trunk you gasped as though something was wrong. Charlotte said, Oh no mom nothings wrong. But she lied to her mom. When the trunk lid came open and Charlotte saw what was there she had the feeling that she had seen it before. She knew already what was there. Almost like she was the one who packed it, but she knew that was impossible, the trunk was over one hundred and thirty years old. Charlotte's mom started going through some of the jewelry and things in the tray built into the lid of the trunk. Charlotte ask her mom to lift up the tray and under it was a old yellowed photograph of a young couple. Charlotte knew in an instant who the couple was. It was her great great aunt Sarah and her fiance. The woman was beautiful and the man, Oh! he was quite handsome. They made a charming couple and as Charlotte looked at the picture she had a sad empty feeling come over her. Her heart was aching as she felt a sadness like she'd never known before and didn't know why. All the while she was in a daze. Her mom was talking to her but she didn't hear a word she was saying. Her mind was in another place and time. Finally her mom grabbed the picture from Charlotte.

Charlotte was shocked she said, why did you do that? Her mom said, Honey, you've been there for ten minutes and done nothing but stare at that picture. Are you o k? Maybe we should give it up and finish another time. Charlotte said, No! I'll be fine and what ever came over her was gone. The women continued to dig deeper in the trunk. They took everything out and looked over each piece until they got to what looked like an old pillow case. It was quite large and it had to be, because inside was a gown. Not an ordinary gown, but a wedding gown and it was beautiful. It was made of lace with a very high lace neck and long lace sleeves that had buttons clear to the elbows. The skirt was made with layers of satin and lace. The gown was beautiful and Charlotte imagined herself wearing the gown. It was extremely elegant and very old fashioned. Under the gown in the trunk was a smaller case and it contained the hat and veil to match the gown. Charlotte laid everything aside and picked up a small flat box from the very bottom of the trunk. She opened the box and found old letters. Love letters! from the captain to his fiancee during the war. Charlotte felt like the letters were sacred and just glanced through the envelopes. She found the farewell letter to Sarah's family with the official letter from the government informing the family of the captains death. Charlotte read the letters out loud and as she did she felt great sorrow.

She looked at her mom with tears in her eyes. Her Mom said, like in the fairy tales, huh? Charlotte said, Yeah! no kidding. So they made a solemn promise that the house would stand empty until they could live in it together, but they're both dead. They don't need the house now. I do and I want it. Charlotte's mom was overwhelmed by her comment. She said, what on earth do you want with that old run down place? Have you seen the inside of the house or do you have any idea what might be there? You might be asking for a lot more than you bargained for girl. Maybe you should just forget the whole idea. Charlotte completely ignored what her mother said. She for some reason has already made up her mind. She wants the house no matter how long or what it takes. She simply has to have it and in the trunk she found names of some of the people who may have had possession of the property after the captain died. Now Charlotte had a place to start her search. That was enough to make her happy for the moment. She was really eager to find out all she could about the captain and his fiancee. Now she had a place to start, but in all the excitement of digging out the trunk Charlotte completely forgot about the diary that her mother talked about. They were gathering everything up to put back in the trunk when Charlotte found it. She touched the diary and instantly felt a chill clear to her bones. She dropped the diary on the floor and just stared at it. Her mother ask her what was wrong. She said, I don't know, but I know I felt something. But that's crazy isn't it? Her mom said,

Honey maybe you should just let the old place go. What is it that's driving you so hard. Are you doing this for you or someone else? Charlotte looked at her mom. She was puzzled by her statement. She said mom, What in the hell are you talking about. Charlotte's mom turned away from Charlotte. When she spoke her voice was soft and shaky. She turned back to Charlotte and said, Honey, there's something I didn't tell you. You know in the letter that Sarah wrote to her family. She said that she and her captain would live in the house together. Well some people believe that she is in the house. Some claim they have even seen her and not only in the house but down by the river. Apparently that's where she lost her life and the people believe, that the couple plan on coming back to be together and live in the house somehow, someday. Charlotte said, Mom I'm not afraid of spirits and if they do come back. It must be gods will. So please quit trying to scare me. I want that house and I want my family to live there. Try to understand when I tell you that I'm willing to find out the truth about the place. And I feel deep in my heart that there is no evil there. As she was speaking she reached down and picked the diary up off the floor. She opened it to the front page and read the first few lines. It didn't take her long to realize that the diary truly belonged to Sarah.

As Charlotte stood with both hands on the diary she began to feel a tingling up both her arms. Almost like a slight electrical current and as she felt the tingle she grew weak in the knees. She fell to the floor next to the trunk and went unconscious. When she came to, her mother was standing over her. Charlotte looked at her mother and said, wow! what happened? She shook her head to try to clear it and her mother reached down to help Charlotte to her feet. She said, honey I don't know what happened. One minute I was talking to you and the next thing I knew your were on the floor. Are you okay? Has this ever happened before? If so maybe you should see a doctor. Charlotte said, mom I'm fine, I must of tripped or something. I guess I'm just clumsy, that's all. Charlotte's mom didn't believe a word she said. She saw the look on her face and her eyes, they seemed to change. She looked like the girl in the picture for just an instant. It was like Charlotte was becoming the girl from the diary. The more she read the more Sarah appeared in Charlotte's face. And her mom knew that she wasn't mistaking. She just saw Sarah in the picture in the trunk. But now she thinks she's gone crazy too. And was thinking that her daughter wasn't the only one with a strong imagination and from that point on everything was pretty much back to normal. Charlotte and her mom got everything put away. She ask her mom if she could borrow some of the old papers that were there.

She wanted some of the names and really wanted to read the diary. Her mom said, of course it,s okay, you'll get everything in the end anyway. Because everything was to be handed down to the next generation. And Charlotte was that generation. The women got everything cleaned up and put away in the attic and Charlotte got all the papers together she needed and headed for home. On the way she was thinking of all the places she had to go to start her search. The City Hall, the Court House and if all else fails, the Library. But before she did anything, she wanted to read the diary and that brought her back to what happened to her in the attic. She thought how crazy it would've sounded if she would've tried to explain to her mom what had happened. Especially what she felt and saw. Charlotte was remembering what took place and thought how strange it all was. She remembered the diary and how she was holding it. The book fell open to one particular page. It read, Dear Diary: Today is Tuesday and started out to be a beautiful day. Joe and I were going over some plans for the house and wedding and after we finished, we drove over to the home sight to see how the construction was going. Everything was going as planned, it was magnificent. When we finished there we drove down by the river to our favorite spot. We walked along the river and took in the scenery. It was a beautiful day and we enjoyed our stroll along the riverbank. We got back to the horse and buggy to head home when we heard horses coming. Joe grabbed my arm and pushed me behind him.

He knew that trouble was headed our way. There were three men and they had been drinking pretty heavily. The loudest and drunkest was known as Auggie Denton. The town drunk and trouble maker.

He was the youngest son of a big rancher on the other side of town. When he got into trouble his daddy always bought him out of it. The men jumped down from their horses and two of them grabbed Joe and tried to hold him and Auggie came at me. Joe tried to get loose but a fight broke out. Fist were flying and the two were getting the best of Joe. Auggie meanwhile grabbed me and tried to kiss me, I fought with everything I had in me, to keep his slimy lips away from mine. As he squeezed me against him, he told me that he's had his eye on me for a long time and said, no other man would have me. He wanted me for his wife. He tried to kiss me again and I bit his lip. He yelled and cursed me and drew back his fist and hit me. The blow was so hard it snapped my neck and blood gushed from my mouth. I screamed in his face that I would rather die than have him touch me. He laughed and said that could happen if you don't do what I want. He laughed again as I spit in his face and he grabbed me again to kiss me. I fought with all my strength and Auggie was getting the best of me. Then the next thing I knew something flew right over top of me. It was Joe, he pulled Auggie away from me. They fought for some time, Auggie didn't give up as easily as the other two did.

Joe was really giving him a beating when finally he ran to his horse and rode off. Joe turned to me and fell to his knees. He was covered with blood but I was his first concern. He ask if I was okay. I told him I was fine and got him to lay on the ground. He was the one who needed attention not me. I tore the bottom of my petty coat to wipe some of the blood away and went to the river to wet it. I turned to go back to Joe, when Auggie came riding back. He was cursing at the two of us and swore it wasn't over as he rode off again. As Charlotte read the pages she started seeing some kind of flashes. In the flashes she saw the face of a man, a gritty dirty man, who was ugly and angry. Charlotte had no idea what it meant and didn't dare say anything to her mom. She wouldn't know what to say anyway. How do you explain something like this. So Charlotte just dismissed the whole episode and got her thoughts back to where she would start her search. She pulled in the driveway to John's parents house. She gathered all the papers and went into the house. She laid everything on the dining room table and went straight to the kitchen to help cook supper. Shortly, John came home. They all sat down to eat and afterwards John and Charlotte went to the dining room to look through the papers that Charlotte got from her mom's house. They decided that the first place to look was the Courthouse and if they had no luck there then they would go to the City Hall and last but not least, they would go to the Library. But they thought surely they would have some records in the recorder of Deeds or in the Record of Wills department. All they were really looking for, were some records of some kind to bring them close to the previous owners.

John took the next day off work. He didn't really feel bad about it because he had several personal days and he used one for what he thought was a good reason. He decided to help Charlotte with the search. He really didn't know why, but he too took a fancy to the big old place. He fell in love with the lay of the land and thought it had a lot of potential. He thought if he helped things would go quicker and maybe they could get into the house without trespassing. They got started early and headed for the Courthouse. Their search started by looking for records from the oldest McMasters in the cemetery. They began the year Aron died and found nothing, so next they tried to remember the year the mother died. When they finally remembered the name and date they started looking in the record books for taxes or anything that would lead them to a present day owner. They found that all the records for that time were very poorly documented and decided that they really had their work cut out for them. After hours of rummaging through old books and documents at the tax office they went to the Record of Wills department. Thinking surely the place was left to an heir in a Will somewhere. There again they started with Aron McMasters and his wife. They searched for hours and went through hundreds of pages.

The Wills that were recorded were in poor condition. The ink was fading and the pages were brittle, not to mention the fact that the penmanship was very poor and barely readable. They were getting really discouraged and were about to give up. When suddenly Charlotte looked at John and said, God! are we dumb. Here we are looking for the owners of the property and we're probably looking for the wrong name. So at this point, John and Charlotte sat down at the table to regroup. They decided that in the Eighteen Hundreds the records are in poor condition, but by the Eighteen Fifties the records were a little more accurate and by that time, Captain Joe McMasters was planning on building a Mansion. So by that time there should be some kind of Land Transfer somewhere and that gave them a time frame to start in. The year was the year her mom told her about. It was the year before the Civil War broke out. So they started in the year of Eighteen Fifty Nine and headed back to the Recorder of Deeds. They went through Year after year and still they had no luck. The records were still in poor condition. They were about to give it up and head for the Library when Charlotte said, Bingo! I think I found something and sure enough she did. She found enough information to get them well on their way to finding the owners. They followed the path of papers in the order of names and dates. Before long they had the name of the only living heir to all the property.

They went to the copy machine and made copies of everything they thought they might need. When they finished with that they headed home. When they got back to the house, they tried to relax and unwind but found it impossible. They were both anxious to start their search and find one Mrs. Wilma Darcy who was the last living relative of the McMasters family. They looked through all the papers they had copied and found that her most recent address was still in Richmond. The next day John went to work but he wasn't doing very well,Things were going slow in the plant, so John ask if he could go home. His boss told him to go and before he left the plant he called home to ask Charlotte what the game plan was for today. She said she would like to find Mrs. Darcy if she could. John said meet me in town and I'll go with you and we'll try to find out as much as we can today. They met at a little diner in town. It was one they used to go to when they were dating. They had breakfast and talked things over. The first thing they wanted to do was find where the lady lived. They ask for directions on how to find Cherry Creek Road. They followed the directions they were given and were just a little surprised when they learned that it took them out past the old place. They drove for three or four miles and found nothing. They rode up and down the road a couple of times but still couldn't find the name of the road. When they finally decided to give up, they saw an old man walking along the road.

John stopped and Charlotte ask him for directions. He told them to turn around and go back until you cross a bridge. When you get over the bridge you see a road to the right, Turn there and follow the road as far as it takes you. You can't miss the place. It's the only house out there. They followed his directions and sure enough, there it was. Clear at the end of a mile long road. When they got close to it Charlotte said, My God look at this place. Do you believe something like this could be found in the middle of nowhere. I had know idea there was places like this still around here. The place was a mansion, it was gigantic and reminded Charlotte of some of the Plantation homes she saw in the movies. The place was elegant, the lawn was beautifully kept and all the shrubs were groomed and cut in different designs. Charlotte thought they looked like green ice sculptures. There was an iron gate at the beginning of the circle driveway. As you followed the driveway to the house. It went right up and around to the front entrance. Across the driveway from the front door was a fountain and in the middle of it was a gigantic statue of a Greek God, it was showing signs of age but never the less, it was magnificent. Charlotte ask John what something like this would cost. He said, he would have to work three life times to be able to afford to just live there.

They parked the car in the driveway in front of the entrance. They walked to the door and used the knocker that was there. They had to use the knocker a couple of time before anyone answered it. Finally when the door opened slowly, a little old lady peeked out. She stayed behind the door and talked from there. She acted as though she was afraid of who was there. Charlotte thought that she didn't blame the woman for being afraid in this day and age. The lady said, can I help you? Charlotte said yes, I hope so, we're looking for a Mrs. Wilma Darcy. Does she live here? The lady said, I'm Mrs. Darcy, state your business. Charlotte said, my husband and I did some research and found that you own some property that we would like to inquire about. The lady slowly backed away from the door and ask John and Charlotte in. As they enter through the doorway Mrs. Darcy apologized for being rude. She said, now a days you can't trust to many people you know. It just ain't safe. Charlotte said, that's quite alright we understand. The lady showed them to her study and Charlotte looked around and was intrigued by the house and the elegant furnishings. Everything was so beautiful and expensive. When they got to the study the lady told them to have a seat and left the room.

John and Charlotte had a seat and waited. They looked over the furniture while she was gone and found most of it was priceless antiques. They admired it very much and had plenty of time to look things over. The lady was gone for ten minutes or so before she came back into the study and in her hands she carried a tray of coffee and cookies. She offered the two coffee and told them to make themselves comfortable.

She said, I'm Wilma Darcy and I'm very glad to meet you. Your name is? And John introduced himself and his wife to the lady. When the conversation got started, they talked about the property and the old house. Mrs. Darcy was intrigued by the young couple. She enjoyed talking to both of them but her main interest was in Charlotte. John noticed that most of the conversation was directed to his wife but really didn't mind. He figured it was because the lady was lonely and enjoyed having another woman to talk to but Charlotte felt like it was more, much more, and didn't know why. Mrs. Darcy came to the point of the conversation where she wanted to know why a young couple like themselves would be interested in an old place like that one. She also told the couple, that no one has ever lived in the house and before them no one ever wanted to. You do know that there are stories about that place. Stories that scare people away. Charlotte said, yes we're aware of the stories and we've even heard a few but we would like to know more. Can you help us? We're really not sure how all the stories come together. All we know is that we really like the place and if your the one we need to see, we'd like to buy it. Mrs. Darcy stared at Charlotte, she sat quietly and looked into her eyes. She studied Charlotte for a few seconds. Charlotte felt real uneasy about the women looking so hard at her.

She felt like she was trying to read something that wasn't there but Charlotte didn't say a word she just sat and looked at John.

Finally Mrs. Darcy reached out and took Charlotte's hand in hers and said, Yes I can help you. For the time is right. Then she said to the couple, do you have time to talk. Charlotte looked at John and he nodded and Mrs. Darcy said good, we'll have some coffee and cookies and I'll try to help you as much as I possibly can. Mrs. Darcy said, there's a lot of things to know about the old McMasters place. You do know, that people swear that the place is haunted, but of course I don't believe it is. I think that what ever goes on out there is for a reason. In all my years I've come to believe that there's a truth to be known out there and when it's found everything will be fine. Mrs. Darcy was the one who did all the talking. The only time John spoke was when Mrs. Darcy directed a question to him. She ask John about his work and his interests in general. She then ask about the children, how many and their ages. She was quite interested in the family as a whole and John by this time was feeling pretty comfortable about the way things were going.

Then suddenly the conversation was directed to Charlotte. The couple found themselves amazed to find out that Mrs. Darcy could tell Charlotte so much about herself. It was like she had known Charlotte all her life and yet they never met before today. The couple just thought it was coincidence and didn't think much of it and finally Charlotte told Mrs. Darcy that she loved the place and would really like to see the inside of the house. Mrs. Darcy quietly stood up and walked out of the room. John and Charlotte sat there looking at each other. They wondered if they said something to upset the old woman. But shortly Mrs. Darcy came back into the room and walked directly to Charlotte. She reached out and took Charlotte's hand and placed the key to the house in it. She said, go to the house and see how you like it, but the most important thing of all is see how you feel there. I really need to know what you feel when you walk through the door. Now, you two youngsters run along. You wore the old lady out and I really need to rest, but come back soon and we'll talk some more. Mrs. Darcy walked the young couple to the door and when Charlotte was going through the doorway Mrs. Darcy reached out and took her by the hand. She squeezed it gently and said, come back soon Dear, and said Good day with a smile and stepped back inside and closed the door. John and Charlotte walked to the car. When they were ready to get in Charlotte took one more look at the door to see if she could see Mrs. Darcy. She couldn't and got in the car and they headed for home. They discussed their visit with the old lady and decided to go to the house Saturday. They figured that way they could take their time and look the place over real good. They figured the place would take a lot of time and money as old as it was and to see just how much it would take to become livable.

They already knew that the house would need plumbing done. Because when the place was built they didn't even know about inside plumbing or inside bathrooms and besides when they were there they saw a little shanty out back and knew it was the outhouse. John and Charlotte got home and they told John's mother about their visit with Mrs. Darcy. As they talked they continued to make plans for Saturday. John's mom wasn't real happy about all of this because she too, knows the stories of the old place. Maybe a little differently, but never the less the stories all lead to the same conclusion. There's just something not right about the place. But the couple didn't care about the stories. They were thrilled to be able to see the inside of the old house and although each one of them felt just a little uneasy about going out there again. They kept their feelings and thoughts to themselves.

Chapter Five

THE MIRROR IMAGE

The next couple of days seemed to drag, almost like time was in slow motion, but finally Saturday came and John and Charlotte were up early and eager to get started. They left the children with John's mom and headed out the door and were on their way to the old house. As they were leaving John's mother said, you two be real careful out there and the couple reassured her they would. As John was driving they joked about everyone being so superstitious. They were both truely excited about the adventure that lies ahead. Soon they came to the lane leading to the house. John turned in the lane and drove the car as far as he could. He parked the car and they both got out. This time they came prepared for anything. John went to the trunk and pulled out a gasoline powered weed cutter. He looked at Charlotte and said, no self respecting ghost will fool with me, I came armed and I'm extremely dangerous. They laughed and joked all they way to the well. With the weed cutter it didn't take long at all to cut a path, and Charlotte stuck to John like glue, she didn't want him to get to far ahead of her. John cleared down to the well and all around the benches. After all that, they sat down on one of the benches. John said, he needed a breather and they sat so he could rest a few minutes. They sat by the well and admired the place. Then John said, Charlotte look at that. Charlotte said, what? John pointed over at the other bench and said, is that roses over there? And sure enough in all the brush stood some of the most beautiful roses they had ever seen. Charlotte was fascinated with their beauty.

She walked over and around the bench to get a closer look. She reached out to touch one and all of a sudden the wind picked up and a cold breeze hit her right in the face. She felt a cold sensation all over her body and as all this was happening she felt dizzy. She shook her head to try to clear it and saw the flashes again. In the flashes she saw the face of a young girl, a very unhappy girl. Charlotte for some reason felt pity for the girl. The next thing she knew was more flashes, only this time she didn't see the girl. She saw a man, a mean looking, ugly man. Charlotte felt fear, she knew that somehow this man was dangerous, but who is he and why am I seeing him? Charlotte was confused and lightheaded. She fell to her knees. John ran to her and ask her what happened. She lied and said, I'm a little dizzy that's all, and John jokingly said, maybe your going to have another baby. Charlotte slapped him and said, very funny. Come on we have work to do, So get your butt moving Mister and so they got back to clearing the walkway to the house. With the help of the weed cutter they were at the porch in no time at all. They both went to the front door and stood staring at each other. Without saying a word, one knew what the other was thinking. They were both a little skeptical, they had no idea what was hidden behind the door. They didn't know what to expect after all the stories they heard and they were a little reluctant now, to go in. They really didn't know what to believe at this point.

Charlotte finally said, well lets do it. We didn't come here to stare at the door, did we? Now that we're here, we might as well go in. John reached down and put the key in the lock. It opened with ease and he swung the door open. The house was totally dark, all you could see from the light of the doorway was the entrance hall. But John came prepared, he had lanterns and flashlights. He knelt down and lit the lanterns. He handed one to Charlotte and lit the other one. When the entrance hall was lit up they were amazed at the sight. Everything was beautiful, a little dusty after all the years but never the less it was beautiful. By this time the furnishings were priceless antiques and in excellent condition. The staircase went up the middle of the entrance hall which in itself could be another room. It was hugh and from the entrance hall the rooms went off to both sides. Straight back the hallway led to another part of the house. Possibly the kitchen was in that direction and they decided to check that out later. For right now they wanted to go through the rooms off of the entrance hall. Charlotte said, should we stick together or go separate ways. John said, maybe we should stay together and see how things go. She said, that suits me just fine. They first went in the room to the right. It was a library or study and there were books everywhere.

Charlotte picked one up and blew all the dust away and as she opened it she discovered it was like brand new. She said, John I can't believe this, these books are like new. Just a little dusty that's all. John said, I believe it, have you looked at the furniture? Everything's beautiful, the wood and the way it's built. The craftsmanship is fantastic. This stuff was worth a fortune in it's day. Charlotte said, well what would it be worth now? John said, I would imagine it would be worth plenty. There all antiques and isn't it strange, that no one ever broke in to vandalize the place or steal anything. There's a fortune sitting here and I'll tell you something right now. We'll never be able to afford this place, unless she takes everything out and we furnish it with our things. Charlotte said, that's probably what she'll do anyway, don't you think? John said, yeah I would imagine. John didn't say much after that point, he was watching Charlotte. She wasn't aware of what she was doing. She went through the room like she had been there before. She was telling John about something he found in the drawer and he didn't even open the drawer yet. She left the room and went to another one across the hall. John followed her and they were talking about the furnishing in it too. Suddenly, Charlotte stopped dead in her tracks, as she looked around she then realized she had been there before. But that was impossible, she never even knew about the place until a month or so ago. She went on through to another room and John was off in a different direction, he realized how silly he was in thinking the way he did.

He knew Charlotte had never been there before and put the thought out of his mind and went back to having the time of his life.

Meanwhile Charlotte was wandering through the house. Each room she went into she felt the same way. Like she had been there before. She finally went to the staircase and as she walked the steps she got a feeling she had done this before. She said to herself; this is getting ridiculous. I've never laid eyes on this place before, so how can I feel this way. She reached the top of the steps and went straight into the room across the hall. She stepped through the doorway and had a weird feeling come over her. She felt as though she had just come home and soon she'd never have to leave again. By this time John was in another part of the house. He was fascinated with the structure of the place. He liked the idea, that each room had a fireplace and the room he was in now had logs stacked and ready to be burnt. He thought the room could use a fire and put some logs in and tried to get a fire going. The room was damp and cold and he didn't have much luck with the fire, he needed papers or some dried leaves to get it going and went outside to find something to start the fire. Charlotte is still in the same room. Which happens to be the master bedroom. It was the largest room in the whole upstairs and was the most beautiful room that she ever saw. The bed was a big canopy bed and the canopy extended down the poles to the floor.

The blankets were turned down like it was waiting for someone to sleep in it. She walked across the room to the dressing table and thought, I must be a sight for sore eyes and sat down to fix her hair, but when she looked into the mirror she screamed. The face looking back at her was not hers, it was the face of a beautiful young woman. Charlotte turned to get away from the mirror. She was scared to death. She didn't know who or why that happened and sure as hell wasn't about to stick around to find out. As she moved away the girl moved exactly as she did. Charlotte stopped and turned back to the mirror. She looked at the face and studied the features. The eyes were beautiful but sad and the mouth was forming words but no sounds were made and then she realized that the girl in the mirror was Sarah. Charlotte in an instant felt extremely sad. She slowly studied the girl in the mirror, she recognized the sorrow in her eyes. Her first impulse was to try and ease the girls pain. She was feeling tremendous pity for this beautiful young girl and felt the need to reach out and touch her. Charlotte at that moment, raised her hand toward the mirror and pressed her palm softly against the glass. Sarah, her mirror image, moved as gracefully as Charlotte. When the hand touched the mirror. It touched from both sides. Sarah was feeling Charlotte and Charlotte was feeling Sarah and for that moment in time they became one.

Charlotte became very weak at the touch. The room filled with a chilling breeze and Charlotte felt a strange tingling feeling all the way up her arm and eventually through out her entire body. She grows extremely weak and finally her body goes limp. She has no control over herself as she sits and stares into the mirror. The girl looks back and Charlotte somehow sensed a peace coming over her and she was right. Sarah is feeling a little more confident, for now she knows that Charlotte is the one she's waited for all those years and peace will surely come as her spirit is finally laid to rest. For years Sarah has roamed aimlessly. Her soul has never found peace. She was cheated out of life at a very young age and know one ever found her body. She was never given a Christian burial and she has unfinished business. The truth needs to be known and her body found or she'll never find peace in the here after and most importantly, she'll never be with her loving Captain, in Eternity. Charlotte slumped over the dressing table, she's grown weaker and still feels the tingling sensation through-out her body. She knows what just took place. She looked in the mirror and saw the face of Sarah looking back. Charlotte knew from that time on that she was there to help Sarah find her peace and Sarah for the first time in years felt that her peace was soon to come. But then something happened. Charlotte saw pain in those eyes again.

She saw a message of some kind but had know idea what was happening. Charlotte stared into Sarah's eyes, she saw darkness and then flashes. The flashes were like a bad movie. In the flashes this time she saw the face of a man. The same man she saw before, he had rage in his eyes and so much hatred. Charlotte gasped and sat straight up. She was terrorized by his face, she knew in her heart that this man is extremely dangerous. Charlotte found herself confused by the flashes. Then all of a sudden they were gone. They went as quickly as they came. Charlotte was completely drained after her ordeal and laid resting her head on the dressing table. When she was a little stronger she raised her head and as she did her eyes caught the mirror again. The image she saw was that of Sarah again. Sarah was weeping and clutching something to her breast. Sarah slowly moved her hands from her breast and Charlotte then saw that she was holding a letter. Sarah read parts of the letter and cried hysterically. She said, No! this must be some kind of mistake. "Joe, you can't leave me", you promised to come home. Sarah sat weeping as her young heart was breaking. She was pleading for God to help her bring Joe home. Finally she said, Joe I can't and won't go on without you. I need you My Dearest, and then the girl in the mirror went silent and slowly faded away. Charlotte reached out her hand to touch the mirror, she called to Sarah but she was gone.

Just at that moment, John came into the bedroom. He said, so there you are. I've been looking all over for you. You had me a little worried, I called and called. Why didn't you answer me? He looked at Charlotte and she extremely pale. He said, are you alright? Charlotte said, of course I am silly. Why wouldn't I be? Then she quickly changed the subject, she didn't want John to know what happened. She really wanted to tell him, but was afraid he wouldn't want the house if he knew and Charlotte really wanted the house. She knew she needed it now more than anything. She needed it even if only to help the lost soul in the mirror. After finding everything they needed, they left and headed straight to Mrs. Darcy's place. As they were walking out the walkway to the car they got back to the well and both stopped dead in their tracks and just stared at each other. They heard the music again, only different this time. It was coming from a different direction. John was really puzzled by the music. He said to Charlotte, where the hell is it coming from? Charlotte answered him calmly and said, I think it's coming from there and pointed in the direction of the cemetery. They stood quietly and listened. John said, God that's weird. Every time I hear it the hair on the back of my neck stands straight up. Charlotte said, That's the most ridiculous thing I ever heard. It's only music, for crying out loud. How can it possibly hurt you. She was having fun with John when she said, Are you afraid a note will fall on you or something. She laughed and John got real upset with her. He said, go ahead and laugh but don't you think there's something a little weird about music playing out in the middle of nowhere.

It's like coming from thin air and not to mention the spooky fact that it seems to be coming out of the middle of the Cemetery. Correct me if I'm wrong, but the last time we heard it, it was coming from inside the house. Right? So how is it, that it's now coming from the cemetery? Charlotte was amused by John's little boy instincts. Like what is that? I'd like to find out but it scares me. She said, Honey don't you think your over reacting just a little? There's nothing to be afraid of. Whatever it is, I'm sure there has to be a logical explanation for it. Maybe it's the little old man, he might be trying to scare us enough for us to leave here. Maybe, he wants the place to himself. John turned to look at Charlotte and said, yeah that's it. You know until now I had forgotten entirely about the spooky little old man and your probably right. Now, John was content for the moment. He said to Charlotte, you know you have to admit the music is pretty damn weird and I've never heard anything quite like it. It must be as ancient as the old man. Charlotte frowned and said, go ahead and make your comments about it. I personally think it's the most beautiful music that I have ever heard. It's so romantic and old fashion and after all it should be. The old man called it The Sweetheart's Waltz and at this point the conversation was dropped. Then suddenly they noticed the music had stopped as quickly as it started.

John and Charlotte got to the car and John started the engine. He began to back out the lane, when Charlotte said, stop and pointed to the direction of the Cemetery. There standing in between the to largest and oldest headstones was the little old man. He never moved, he just stood and stared as they backed out of the lane. Well needless to say that really made John's day. He was beginning to be a little reluctant about the place. He was starting to think it was haunted, but now he knows that what ever happened there. The little old man played a big part in and now he feels for sure that the old man was trying to scare them off. John, backed down and on to the road. He started to pull out and head towards home when all of a sudden he slammed on the brakes. Charlotte went flying and she hit her head on the windshield. She looked at John and said, are you crazy. What the hell's wrong with you? John without explanation, backed the car up and pulled back in the lane and went up to the top of the knoll. Charlotte said, What in the hell got in to you? Your driving like a wild man. John didn't answer her. He stopped the car, jumped out and ran to the front of the car. There he stood as tall as he could and paraded like a rooster. He yelled down to the old man. This place will be ours, no matter what it takes. You can't scare me off, you old goat. Then he must of felt better because he turned and got back into the car and drove off.

Now that their on their way again. They went to Mrs. Darcy's to drop off the key and while they were there, they decided to get all the particulars of the place. As they drove up the circle drive, Mrs. Darcy was standing at the door to meet them. She said, I assume you were at the house. Is that right? John said; yes we just came from there and we wanted to give the key back to you right away. Mrs. Darcy smiled and said, you really didn't have to hurry. I knew right away that the both of you were trust worthy and I can spot an honest person a mile away. As she spoke, she invited the couple in. She lead them to the sitting room and on the table sat a tea pot filled with tea. Along with the tea were three cups and saucers. Everything was ready and waiting as though she was expecting them. John picked up on this right away. He said to himself, how in the hell, did this woman know we were coming? It puzzled him and Mrs. Darcy looked at John and read what he was thinking. She smiled a broad smile and said to John. No dear, I didn't know you were coming. I was expecting guest and they canceled just before you pulled in. It was a close lady friend whom I've known since I was a girl. She's been ailing, and this morning she took a turn for the worse. I just recieved the call before you drove up. She smiled again and said to John. No I'm not physic or anything like that. John, awkwardly smiled back at her.

He was feeling a little embarrassed to think she knew what he was thinking, but of course he managed to recover pretty quick. Mrs. Darcy was an excellent hostess. She made sure everyone was comfortable before getting into any conversation. She finally sat down and said, well you two, I want to know everything about the old place. I've been wanting to see it but just can't bring myself to go there. I'm just to old I guess and as she was talking she grabbed a pad and pencil as though she was going to take notes. While they talked she wrote down things that really interested her. She was interested in every little detail, no matter how big or small and the three of them talked for a couple of hours. Then the subject of the music came up. When Charlotte began to talk about the music, Mrs. Darcy put down her pencil and stared out the window. John said, Mrs. Darcy are you alright? But she sat there quietly and was thinking of all the things that were handed down through the generations and how she would know when the time was right to give up the property. The music was a sign and she knew at that point that Charlotte was the one it was to be handed to.

Now that Mrs. Darcy knew that Charlotte was the one, she had to be very careful. She didn't want to say anything to scare the couple off. So she thought she would be very tactful in the subject. She ask the couple how well they liked the place. Charlotte immediately answered, I love it, there's so much old fashioned charm there. The place has character and lots of it. If we lived there the only thing that would be changed is the plumbing, in which of course there isn't any. Mrs. Darcy sat and thought a minute. Then she directed her next question to John. She said, John you haven't said a word about the place. What about you, would you be happy there? John said; of course I'd be happy there. The place needs a lot of tender loving care and major cleaning but yes, I would love to call it home. Then John said; Mrs. Darcy the reason we looked you up was so we could talk to you about buying the place and we were hoping you would consider selling the old house and a little bit of land. If not, that would be okay but we would really like to buy the house. Mrs. Darcy said; you know kids I have really enjoyed your company. At my age I tire easily and right now I'm exhausted. So if you two will please excuse me, I'll rest and consider all the possibilities of you buying the place. I have a lot of old papers to go through and they have been buried for years or ages are more like it. So you see you'll have to give me some time. But I will be in touch so leave your name and number please and Charlotte jotted down the information for Mrs. Darcy and they said good day to her.

John and Charlotte got in the car a drove down the driveway. Charlotte noticed that Mrs. Darcy watched until they drove out of sight but what she didn't know was the visit they had with Mrs. Darcy told her exactly what she needed to know. Now she just had to make sure she did everything the right way. She certainly didn't want any restless spirits coming back to her because she over looked some small detail. In the generations before Mrs. Darcy, her family was a spiritual family and in their beliefs. If a person loves someone in life then they will be together in eternity and if for some reason that person is cheated out of life and love. Then the spirits linger until they can reunite with their loved ones to be together through all eternity. And this is exactly what happened to Sarah and Joe. They were robbed but the mystery remains until this day. How did these deaths occur. Was it God's will or the hand of man that chose their fate. The answers lie in the old place and they need to be found and Mrs. Darcy knows that now the time has come to reunite the spirits of the young lovers and to finally put them to rest for all eternity. Their poor souls have suffered and wandered aimlessly, long enough. Mrs. Darcy has to get busy, she's exhausted but she has a lot of old records and papers to go through. She went directly to her study. When she got to her book case she reached up to the top shelf and pulled down a book. The book was bound in black velvet and trimmed in gold. She looked at the book and held it for a short time, then she sat down and opened it.

At the very beginning of the book there was a picture of Joe and Sarah, they made a beautiful couple and the picture was taken the day they announced their engagement. After Mrs. Darcy looked at the picture she slowly turned the old crisp pages being very careful not to damage them. Finally she came to the page she was looking for. At the beginning of the page it read. I have grown to be a young man and still I'm being tormented by the same dreadful dream. In my dream it's dark and very damp and cold. The air is so heavy that it's hard to breath. In the sky there are flashes of lightning and the sound of thunder off at a distance. It's strange though it's not raining and then I realize the air is so heavy because it's filled with smoke. There are men all around and their screaming and yelling. Everyone's in a panic and I don't know why. The thunder seems to be getting closer and then suddenly I realize, the thunder, isn't thunder at all. It's the sound of guns and I find myself in the midst of a horrible battle. I'm soon standing face to face with the enemy and suddenly something hits me hard from behind. I fell flat on my face in a pool of mud. I couldn't breath and then I realized I had to roll over to free my face from the sludge. When I freed my face from the slime I saw a shadow hovering over me. I wiped the mud and muck from my eyes and saw three men standing over me. They were laughing, my falling was a joke to them. I reached up for their hands, but they only laughed as they pushed my head back in the mud. I was suffocating and they got great pleasure out of my suffering. I was dying and my death was a joke. I heard them whispering and laughing and again like all the other dreams, I wake up scared out of my wits.

I feel that my dreams are a premonition and that my life will end at the hands of these three men, whoever they are. I don't know where or why but I feel sure that's my destination. If this is the way my life should end, the truth needs to be known. I will never be able to rest knowing that someone took my life and not knowing why. My spirit will never be at peace until the truth is known.

Mrs. Darcy finished reading the passage from the book and closed it gently and then reached for another book. "A diary". This diary belonged to Joe's mother. The pages were tattered and torn but still readable, so she slowly leafed through to the date of Joe's death. On that page she found the official letter that was handed to Joe's parents when Joe was killed. The letter stated that Joe was a fine officer and a gentleman and he served his country well. He died for a cause he truely believed in. Then they closed the letter by sending their deepest regrets that they had to inform the family of their sons death. After grieving over her son, Joe's mother had a gut feeling that something just wasn't right about Joe's death. She knew in her heart that there was something wrong, but had no idea what. She suspected that his death was not due to the battle. She felt sure he died at the hands of someone evil.

Joe's mother contacted his Commanding Officer and insisted that they run an investigation on Joe's death. She told him that she suspected that Joe had been murdered. The man was very reluctant but finally agreed. Joe's mother was satisfied for now and went on with her life thinking that the truth would be found. But the fact is, that the officer she spoke with had a war to fight and the matter of Joe's death got pushed aside and then finally forgotten. So the mystery of his death still remains a mystery. Joe's mother was in great despair. She believed too, that if the truth wasn't found that Joe would never be at peace. And she vowed that day, that if it took the rest of her life she would try to find the truth. Mrs. Darcy read the diary until she was totally exhausted. She decided to rest and look for the papers for the house tomorrow. She left the study and went to her bedroom to relax in her easy chair. She sat down and covered her legs with a lap throw and sat and looked out the bedroom window looking out over the grounds. She always enjoyed the beauty of her gardens and as she sat there and relaxed she began to doze and soon she was drifting in a peaceful sleep. Soon she entered into a dream state and in her dream, There was a handsome young man walking towards her. He's very happy to see her as he smiles and extends his arms to her. She walked to him and as they embraced. He said, I've waited a long time to see you. He stepped away and looked deep into the her eyes and said, now is the time.

He smiled and then slowly drifted away. Mrs. Darcy woke with a jolt and she knew in an instant what the dream had meant. She knew that the young man was Joe and that he came to her so she would know that the time is right. Now she had to turn the property over to the young couple. She now knows that Charlotte's destination is to free the tortured souls.

Chapter Six

HOME AT LAST

The next morning was a beautiful day, the sun was shining bright and the day was warm. John had just left for work when the phone rang. Charlotte answered and Mrs. Darcy was on the line. She said, hello Charlotte, I hope it,s not to early. I'm calling to ask you and your husband to come see me as soon as you can. Preferably this evening. You will try to make it, won't you? Charlotte was excited. She said, we'll be there. Mrs. Darcy said, good I'll see you later, about seven will be fine and she hung up the phone.

Charlotte called John at work, she was so excited she could hardly talk. John patiently waited and listened to her ramble on and on. He couldn't get a word in edge ways and finally Charlotte finished and John told her, yes they would go and told her he had a lot of work to do and said, I love you. I'll talk to you later and hung up the phone. For Charlotte the day seemed to drag, she was getting very impatient. She really was anxcious to find out what Mrs. Darcy had to say. But all the time she had the feeling that everything was going to work out. So, she made herself busy to pass the time until John came home, but she really couldn't think of anything else.

Finally, it was time for John to come home. He pulled into the driveway and ran to the house. It was pretty close to six and he had to get cleaned up. He said hello to everyone and went to take a shower.

He didn't have time to eat supper so Charlotte made him some sandwiches to take with them. On the way to Mrs. Darcy's house, they discussed the fact that Mrs. Darcy may not want to sell the place. Then they were feeling a little depressed and decided to wait to find out before they got all bummed out. They pulled into the driveway and drove up to the entrance to the house. Charlotte enjoyed being at the place, it was so beautiful. They got out of the car and went to the door and rang the bell. Almost immediately, Mrs. Darcy opened it. She smiled at them and invited them in to the sitting room. She had been prepared for their visit, she had tea on the table and cookies on a platter beside the tea. She poured three cups of tea and handed John and Charlotte theirs.

When she took care of her guests she got hers and sat down to talk business. Before she got started, she sipped her tea and said, you know I really enjoy a good cup of tea when I have good company to share it with. She looked at Charlotte and then at John and said, I think I might be able to help the two of you. She sipped her tea once again and sat the cup on it's saucer. I decided to sell the property to you. It's not really doing me any good and it just sits there. It's costing me money in taxes that I could be using somewhere else. And besides that, it would make a beautiful home for someone and I'm to old to fool with it. The couple couldn't believe their ears. They were so excited about the news and then realized she didn't tell them how much. But Mrs. Darcy put them at ease real quick. She made them an offer that they couldn't refuse, but John was a little skeptical when he heard the price. He said to her, why so cheap? We're willing to pay a fair price for the place. We don't want someone to give us anything. Mrs. Darcy sat and stared at her cup. She sipped her tea once again and said, My dear young man, I'm an old woman. I have only one living relative and he surely won't be needing that place. You see he has all of this and much, much more to inherit. He really won't have much need for any of this. You see he lives like a hermit somewhere down by the river. His mind is not good, he thinks he is the care taker for the river.

He clears debris from the banks and cleans everything up for miles. He's done that for years. The people around here, seem to think that he should have been put somewhere in a home for the

Mentally disturbed. But they don't know him, he's totally harmless. He thinks that he,s God's handyman. That's all that he thinks about and in his mind he lives out there where he thinks he does the most good. So you see, he won't be needing it. She said, look around you. He won't have much use for any of this either. So Please, don't get the wrong idea. That's why, I decided to sell it so cheap. I like the idea of a family living there and the house and grounds could use some tender loving care. Now after what I just told you, do you think my brother would miss the place? John looked at Charlotte and they both looked at Mrs. Darcy and shook their heads no. Mrs. Darcy was delighted and she said, good then it's settled. Right?

Charlotte said, I want that house more than anything and then John said, ok, we'll take it. And the matter was settled. It took about two weeks to get the paper work done. The following weekend, John and Charlotte started to make arrangements to move in. They called in both families to help clean up the place. Finally after a lot of soap and water, dusting and vacuuming. The place was clean enough to move in to.

The very first thing John and his dad had to do was hook up a generator. There was no electricity in the house. The vacuum and other cleaning appliances ran on electricity so they really needed the generator. Personally John and Charlotte liked the idea of not having electricity, they thought everything was authentic that way. But they decided the children needed it to watch TV. and light to do their homework and the gas lights were inadequate for that type of thing. Not to mention, the children's eyes would go bad from poor lighting. So, first things first. They called an electrician to do the wiring and a plumber to do the plumbing and install the bathrooms. Those were the two most important jobs for the time being. Around the house things got pretty hectic. Plumbers and electricians were everywhere and things got really confusing, but before long the work was done and the house was ready to be occupied. A week later John and Charlotte walked into their new and very elegant home. Although it would take some time for them to feel at home there. It was hugh compared to what they were used to. They were all crammed in the little house of John's parents and there was always someone waiting for the bathroom.

But never the less, it was their home until now. But to their surprise, they took to the place very easily and with good reason.

The house had charm and was extremely warm and cozy. It would be hard to imagine anyone living in a place so beautiful, without being comfortable. The furnishing were the finest to be made in that era and John and Charlotte decided to leave everything the way it was originally. The place was filled with some of the finest antiques and collectibles that a person could ever imagine and everything there stayed where Sarah put it all those years ago. Nothing changed except the kitchen and the bathrooms. But for the most part the house is exactly the way it was over a hundred years ago. It didn't take John and Charlotte long to realize how lucky they were. But Charlotte knew that luck had nothing to do with it. It was fate that brought them there and for some reason and somehow she feels like she has finally come home at last. John and Charlotte have been so busy with their work that time has simply flown by. The holidays are just around the corner and the hustle and bustle of getting things organized is almost finished. John has been real busy on the outside while Charlotte has been occupied in the house. She's putting some of the finishing touches to the house. She's cleaned all the fireplaces to get them ready for winter while John was trying to finish the driveway. Charlotte just finished in the living room when she noticed the machine outside stopped running.

She headed to the entrance hall and almost got to the front door when she was struck with severe pain in her head. It was so great that she dropped to her knees, she was extremely nauseated. The pain felt like something hit her from behind but there was nothing there that could have caused a blow. She slowly struggled to her feet and braced herself up with the table in the entrance way. She looked up and saw herself in the mirror over the table. Her eyes were blurred as she saw herself fading away and Sarah took form right before her eyes. Sarah has returned once again only this time she was covered in blood. She looks as though she had been beaten, her head had a Hugh cut on it and blood was squirting from the wound. Sarah was trying to speak but no words would come. Charlotte struggling to keep herself on her feet stood and watched the young girl. She felt great pity for Sarah. She has been hurt badly and possibly this was the time when she died. If the wounds didn't kill her then the loss of blood may have. She was bleeding everywhere. The sight was horrifying to Charlotte, all she could do was stand there and watch and as she did she grew weaker. She grabbed the table even harder to hang on but it was no use. She collapsed and fell to the floor. The machine was quiet outside because John shut it down. He needed a break, he was hungry and thirsty and went to the house to get what he wanted. He entered the house from the back door.

The children were out playing and the house was quiet. He thought, that's strange the house is so quiet it was almost eerie. The house had a feeling of cold emptiness but John shrugged the feeling and went on the search for Charlotte. He called to Charlotte but everything was quiet. He called again and went through the kitchen to look for her. He went through the door to the hallway and called her name once again. On his way through he looked up to the second floor through the railings. He saw no signs of Charlotte up there and went in through the hall towards the entrance. As he walked down the hall, he looked into the study to see if she was in there but with no luck. John slowly turned to go to the living room and as he did his heart dropped, he saw his wife lying in the shadows on the floor. She looked lifeless as he ran to her and soon he saw that she was breathing. At that point he felt some relief but he still had to find out what happened. He knew she couldn't have fallen down the steps. She was to far away, but what could have happened to her. John knelt down and slowly but carefully raised Charlotte from the floor. He rested her head in his lap as he tapped her cheeks to get her to come around. She raised her hands to her head and moaned as though she was in extreme pain as she opened her eyes. When she looked up at her husband she didn't recognize him right away. She paniced and tried to pull away. Charlotte still being mostly Sarah, didn't recognize him. John struggled with Charlotte while she hit and kicked him but he didn't give in to her.

He kept calling her name and finally Sarah slowly slipped away and Charlotte became herself again. Charlotte looked up at John and said, "Wow" what happened? John said, I don't know, I was hoping you could tell me. Are you alright? She said, yes I think so but I don't remember what happened. All I can remember is that I was coming to see why the machine stopped running. Then I got a severe pain in my head and now I find myself lying on the floor. Charlotte was thinking that something serious was happening to her. She was feeling panic inside and was afraid she was losing her grip on reality. John was very concerned about Charlotte. He ask if she thought she should see a doctor. The headaches scared him, he thought she could have a blood clot passing to the brain or all kinds of terrible things that could cause such pain and asked once again. Do you need to go to the doctor's? Knowing in his heart what the answer would be. So he helped her to her feet. She was feeling a little woozy when she stood up and somehow felt a little different. Like she just wasn't herself. John helped Charlotte to the living room and sat her on the sofa. He got her some water and she drank almost the whole glass. She laid back and closed her eyes for a short time and John thought that she fell asleep. So he sat quietly and thought about what would happen if Charlotte was to become sick in some way or maybe even worse. He decided to push those kind of thoughts out of his head.

He didn't even want to think about what life would be without Charlotte being there. Charlotte opened her eyes and looked at John. He said, I thought you were sleeping. Charlotte being exhausted from her ordeal, told John that she just wanted to go lay down a crossed the bed for awhile. She ask if he would watch the kids and he said, sure you rest. He walked her up the steps and helped her on to the bed. When she got comfortable he covered her with a quilt and kissed her. He said, rest for awhile and everything will be fine. He walked from the room and closed the door and as he was going down the steps he turned to look at the bedroom door. He was truly worried about Charlotte. The bedroom was quiet and Charlotte fell asleep as soon as she hit the bed. She slept a peaceful sleep for at least two hours and when she finally woke she looked at the clock and realized it was way past supper time. She said, good grief, I have a family to feed. So she got up and went straight to the kitchen. John was in the kitchen when she got there. He had supper already underway and was singing in the process. The singing helped him keep his mind occupied.

John turned when Charlotte came to the kitchen. He said, How are you feeling? She said, better, I guess I was just tired and needed to rest. John said, Great! I'm glad to hear it and while he was peeling potatoes he said, Guess what? Charlotte said, What? He said, while you were sleeping, I took the kids and we went for a walk out through the old cemetery. Guess what we found? Charlotte said, What did you find? He said, We walked all the way through the cemetery and got back far enough to see the tomb. We looked out and found the little old man sitting right in front of the door to the Tomb. Then he proceeded to say, at first he really freaked me out. I wasn't prepared to meet anyone out there, but then I decided to find out what he was doing there. I said to him, Who are you and what are you doing here? He was reluctant to answer but finally he spoke to me. He said, My dear man. I come to this place all the time. I look after this here place so's no one bothers anything. I watches the house too, till you and your Missus moved in and took over. He said to John, you like it here? John said quickly, Yes, we love it. The man then stood up to walk away and said, Good. Bout time for things here to come to rest and John felt an eerie feeling come over him. He said to the man. What do you mean, what has to come to rest? The little old man continued to walk away and never spoke another word as he disappeared into the woods.

John stood and watched the man walk out through the woods until he was clear out of sight. He got the impression that something wasn't quite right about the old man. He made John feel really uneasy and he didn't have the slightest idea why. John turned to Charlotte and said, "God" He's spooky. He makes me nervous and I really don't like the idea that he hangs around here. When I see him again I'm going to tell him to stay the hell away from the house. Charlotte said, John don't you think your overreacting just a little? John said, not at all. He gives me the creeps. Charlotte said, but he's an old man. What can he hurt? He's probably lonely and has nothing better to do. So how can he possibly hurt you? John didn't hear a word that Charlotte said. He was in deep thought. Then all of a sudden he said, I got it. It's his eyes and the way he looked at me. It was like he knows something we don't. But what and why does he hang around the old cemetery? Charlotte sat quietly while John talked. When he was finished she said once again. Maybe he has no family or anyone and has nothing better to do. Maybe he enjoys walking through the woods and stopped to rest by the tomb. John looked at Charlotte square in the eyes and said, No, there more to it than that. I can feel it and I'm going to find out what it is. The next time I see him, I'm going to follow him and find out what it is that he's up to.

Charlotte got up from the table and walked over to the sink. She stood there and looked out the window towards the cemetery. She turned to look at John and said, do you realize how "ridiculous you sound right now?" God! You sound like a little kid, for crying out loud. But if that's what make you happy, go ahead and do it. John looked at Charlotte. She knew the instant he looked into her eyes that she made him furious. But she couldn't help herself. He was acting like a child and he knew it. At that point Charlotte knew not to say another word and she didn't. The whole conversation came to an end as John stormed out of the kitchen. Charlotte finished cooking supper and called everyone in to eat. John was still out on the porch cooling off when Charlotte went to call him in. She walked over to him and he turned his back on her. She said, Honey I'm sorry, if I upset you. But just take a couple minutes to think about what you said. We've been here for sometime and he hasn't bothered us in any way. I,m not afraid of him. I agree, he is a little spooky but maybe he thinks we are too.

John slowly started to mellow. He looked at Charlotte and realized she was right. How could this old man hurt them as long as they kept an eye on the kids. They didn't have anything to worry about. But John was also thinking, that if the old man ever tried to hurt one of his family he would kill him without even thinking twice about it. Charlotte took John by the hand and led him into the kitchen. By this time John was cooled down but during their meal they chose their conversation very carefully. Trying very hard not to upset each other. They were soon smiling and laughing at the children and they realized how silly they both had been. After that the evening had started to go a lot smoother.

Chapter Seven

THE CAPTAIN RETURNS

Charlotte finished the dishes while John and the kids went to the living room to watch the news. When everything was cleaned up she joined them. The evening went pretty good considering all the hassle that afternoon. John was in a very good mood and Charlotte went along with it. She was enjoying the evening. Around nine o"clock, John told the kids to get their baths and get ready for bed. When they left the room Charlotte slid over beside John to cuddle. John liked the idea very much and before long his male instincts were arousing. He reached his hand down and slid it up under Charlotte's blouse. He gently rubbed and caressed her soft breast. They were in the heat of passion and John gently laid Charlotte back on the sofa. He kissed her and said he would be right back he was going to get the kids in bed. He said, I love you and don't you move. I'll be right back. John stood up and started to walk away. Charlotte laid back her head and closed her eyes. She was feeling very passionate and didn't want to spoil the mood.

Suddenly shes at bolt upright on the sofa. John was screaming and she had know idea what was happening. She heard him say, You Son Of A Bitch: What the hell do you think your doing. John was on his way out into the hall and headed for the door. When he turned and told Charlotte that the old man was peeking in the window at them. He said, if I catch the old Bastard I'll kill him. He won't sneak around here anymore, that's for sure. Charlotte was beside herself, she had no idea what John was talking about. So she followed him to the porch to see what was going on and watched John as he ran into the night. John ran around the side of the house to the window where he saw the old man with his face pressed against the glass. By the time John got there he was gone. John looked around and heard the crisp sound of leaves as the old man ran towards the cemetery. John ran to catch him. The old man didn't run very well. So by the time he got to the tomb John caught him and wrestled him to the ground. John was very angry. But still he was careful not to really hurt the man. When the old man relaxed out of exhaustion, John helped him to his feet. He said to the man, come on your going with me. The old man said, where, where are we goin? John said, shout up and come on. John half dragged the man to the house. The closer they got, the more the man fought.

He struggled desperately. He didn't way any part of the house. When John got to the porch, he saw the old man in the light. He was terrified. John said, what's your problem? You didn't seen to afraid when you were peeping in on us and at this point John reached down and turned the door knob and swung the door open. He pushed the old man inside and he fell to his knees. He had his head tucked in tight against his chest and wouldn't raise it. Charlotte came running to the entrance. She asked John, what was going on. John said, look and pointed to the old man. He said, he was snooping. I saw him with his face pressed against the glass. He was watching us in the living room. Charlotte felt flushed, she was embarrassed knowing someone was watching them. She said, why? John said, I don't know why, but call the police. He's trespassing. Charlotte went to the phone to do what John told her, but she was reluctant to dial the number. She stood for a few minutes and listened. The man was pleading with John not to call the police and said, if you let me go back outside I'll tell you why I'm here. John said, okay but don't try anything funny. You got that? The old man said, okay. John took the old man by the arm and led him outside. The old man was instantly at ease. He wanted no parts

MARGARET TEEGARDEN

of being inside the house and that troubled John. John took the man over to a chair and said, sit down and start talking.

Charlotte followed the guys out on the porch. She grabbed a jacket on her way because the night was cold. She sat down on the chair opposite the old man. She just watched him as he sat with his head hanging. She was feeling pity for the little man. He doesn't look like the type to be dangerous. But then she too, was wandering why he was here and what's he up to? The old man slowly raised his head, he said to Charlotte, I'm sorry ma'am I didn't mean to snoop. I just worry about you in this old place. John said, "Bullshit", we've been here for months and everything's been going well. The old man looked at John and in the moonlight his face softened. He had a sincere and gentleness about him. He said to John, If you listen I'll explain. John said, start talking, I'm listening and I have all night. The old man said, before I tell you why I'm here can you tell me if anything has happened in the house. John was getting angry again and Charlotte dropped her to look away. She knew what was happening He said, Old man, I don't know what your up to but this better be good. The old man said to John, young man please understand I'm not hear to hurt you and yours. I came to warn you and John said, warn us about what? The old man said, It's coming that time again. The anniversary date of the death of the Captain and three day later the girl disappeared. John said, What's that got to do with us? The old man said, alot and continued to say, can't you feel it?

The energy. It's building and getting stronger. I've watched it for years and every year it gets more powerful. John said, your crazy old man. I don't feel anything, but Charlotte never said a word. She knows, she's felt it when she looked in the mirror and she knows Sarah is wanting to come through. But John has no idea what's happened. Charlotte never told him. Charlotte said to John, let him speak. The old man said, Do you know about the Captain and his lady? John said, Yeah, I think, but what's your story? The old man says here goes. Now please listen and don't interupt. John was a little huffy, but he listened anyway. You see I'm the Great Uncle of Mrs. Darcy's I have been cast out of the family for years. Because I'm different. They think I'm crazy. but I'm not. I have a power that they don't understand and I can't blame them, I don't understand it either. I can talk to the dead and they talk to me. I don't really know how or why but that's how it is. Wait let me start from the beginning. When I was a boy about six or so I used to come across the field from out thar and he pointed out past the cemetery. My folks had a house there once. It burnt down some years back. While I lived there I played in the cemetery. I wasn't afraid thar. I had some of my best years right out thar.

Then one day when I was about ten years old, I was sitting out by the tomb. O.K.! people said it was haunted, but I played thar all the time. So I didn't believe them. They were just talkin. But one day in particular at this time of year, I played real hard, I got tired and sat down by the tomb. I sat quiet and just watched the chipmunks running through the headstones. Then I heard someone whisper my name. The voice said, Jessie. It was spooky. The voice was eerie and stretched my name way out. Jessie, help me Jessie. I ran and ran but the voice followed me. I was so scared I peed my pants. I fell in the brush and the voice called to me once more. Jessie don't be afraid, I won't hurt you. So I answered it and that was the day I started to make communication with the dead. The voice was the spirit of Captain Joe McMasters. His spirit is restless and angry. He wants to be at peace to be with his Sarah. But as the years go by it gets harder and harder for this to happen. You see Joe's spirit is restless in the cemetery and Sarah's spirit is restless in the house and gardens. The two are angry spirits. They wander aimlessly through the two areas. They're building a wall of negative energy with all their anger and restlessness. The spirits want to be together, but you see this is impossible. The only way the wall of energy can be destroyed is by truth and no one knows the truth.

The spirits of Joe and Sarah are the only one's who know the real truth and they're both trying desperately to break through the energy field to communicate with someone who can help them to find there peace. And let the truth be known and you my dear people are the one's who were chosen to help them fulfill their needs. John was sitting on the railing of the porch. When the old man finished his story, John jumped up and said, that's the most ridiculous story I ever heard. You are a crazy old man and all your trying to do is scare us off. Well it won't work, you can't scare us off. We love this place and we're not leaving, so you get your ass, off my porch and out of my sight before I have you thrown in jail. The old man said, please sir! I'm trying to help you. The only way you can live here is to help free the spirits. If you don't believe or won't help you could put you and yours in real danger. John said, "bullshit" enough of the spook stories, get out of here. John grabbed the old man and shoved him down the steps to the walkway. It was dark the old man stumbled and fell and as he hit the ground a flash of light came from the old cemetery. John and Charlotte stood and watched as they witnessed the tomb illuminating. It lit up in a gloomy blue green haze and soon floating from the mist was the form of a human being. The form floated to the entrance of the cemetery and slowly descended to the ground. The figure was close enough now for John and Charlotte to see.

It was transparent, but soon you could make out the details of the form. It was a man, he was dressed in a confederate officers uniform and they realized it was the spirit of Captain Joe McMasters. He just stood and stared towards the house. He didn't move until he raised his hands towards Charlotte and motioned for her to come to him. But Charlotte was scared out of her wits. She stood completely still and began to tremble. Something inside her wanted to run to him but she couldn't. She finally fell to the ground as she fainted. John ran to her and picked her head and shoulders off the ground. He looked back towards the cemetery and the aspiration vanished. The old man got up from the ground. He ran to the cemetery and about half way, he turned and said to John, I tried to warn you. Now you handle it. He's madder than he's ever been and the old man ran out of sight into the night. John got Charlotte to her feet and back in the house. They were both really shook up over what just happened. They went to the kitchen and had some coffee. Charlotte was still a little light headed, but felt okay. John on the other hand was really shook up. He's trying to make some sense out of all this. But even after what he just saw he couldn't believe what had happened. He and Charlotte sat at the table and talked about it until close to midnight. Then finally they decided to turn in.

Chapter Eight

THE ROSE GARDEN

When they went to bed they both fell right into sleep. Charlotte was in a restless sleep. She tossed and turned and then finally she entered into a dream state. She saw a young girl running by a river of water. She was beautiful in the sunlight and happy. There was a man chasing her. They were playing and chasing each other. Then the girl became terrified. The handsome young man turned into the nasty ugly man that Charlotte saw in her flashes. He was chasing the girl. She ran and ran until finally he caught her. He grabbed her by her hair and pushed her to the ground. The girl fought with all her strength. The man was angry. He hit her a crossed her head and suddenly Charlotte woke up. She was shaking all over and sweaty and she knew she saw the face before. Charlotte just laid there wide awake and scared to death. She couldn't stop thinking about the dream.

She finally realized that Sarah was murdered by that man. But who is he and where did he put the body. Why did no one ever find out? Charlotte needed some answers. She is now catching on to what's happening. She lays in bed and her mind races until sleep finally comes. The next morning Charlotte woke before the alarm went off. John had to go into the plant early. He helped bring in some wood for the fireplaces and off he went. Now to get the children off and then she could start searching for some of the answers she wanted. She put the children on the bus and head straight out to the cemetery. She wanted to follow the path that might lead her to the old man. She got half way through the stones in the cemetery and looked up to see the tomb. She remembered the night before when the captain appeared to them and thought he was trying to say something to her. But what? Why did he want me to come to him? But she pushed the thought aside and followed the path. It led her deep into the woods. Charlotte felt a little spooked by the trees and the noises she heard but continued on. The path was well worn and easy to follow. Soon she came to a clearing. She stopped to get her breath and looked across. She saw the remains of the old house that the old man said had burned down. She continued across the path until she got to the ruins. Once she got there the path ended abruptly. Charlotte was puzzled. The path just stopped.

She looked up over the weeds and brush to see how to go on. But it was so thick that she decided to turn and go back. As she turned she heard someone calling her name. She turned back around and saw the little old man materialize right in front of her. She was so scared she jumped and fell. She tried to scramble to her feet, but fell again. Her heart was pounding and her chest hurt. She started to cry. She couldn't take the fear. The old man spoke softly to her. He said, Charlotte we need you. Help us, please. Charlotte collected herself a little. She's calmer now, but still she can't think straight. She got to her feet and turned to walk away. She moved slow she was so scared she could just die. But the man called to her again. Charlotte please, he was pleading with her and said, I'm not here to hurt you. I can help. Charlotte turned to look at him. He said, we need you, help us. Charlotte said, what can I do? I'm a mere human, how can I help? The man said, you can help Sarah. She needs your physical form to break through the wall of energy. Until she does, the wall gets bigger and stronger and if it gets much stronger her soul along with Joe's will be lost in time forever. To roam with no hope of ever being at rest. Help them find each other? They need you. Open you mind to her and let her slip in, She's kind and loving and she won't hurt you.

You see Charlotte, she's tried to make contact before. But your body won't totally except her.

She's grown weak by her efforts and when she gets enough energy she'll try again. She knows her love is waiting on the other side of the wall of energy. Now that they created the wall with all their negative energy. They can't penetrate it without your help. If you except Sarah's soul and let the truth be known about their deaths the wall will weaken and Joe will be able to cross over to her and when this happens they will be at peace. Charlotte stood and listened carefully to his every word. She felt pity in her heart for Sarah and her loved one and when the man finished talking he turned into a vapor and disappeared. Charlotte was in total disbelief she turned and ran back the path as fast as she could. She stumbled and fell several times she got cuts and bruises all over her. Finally she broke through the woods at the edge of the cemetery. She looked over and saw the tomb and the Captain was standing at the door. Charlotte panicked, she ran and stumbled and fell against a head stone. She pulled herself up and as she backed away she freaked. The stone she fell against read, Jessie McMasters, died in 1902, the twin of Joseph Owen McMasters. Charlotte said, My God, a ghost. The old man's dead too. Charlotte got to her feet as quick as she could. She turned to the tomb to get a quick look and the Captain and the old man were both standing there in front of the tomb entrance.

Charlotte ran without stopping to the house. She had never been so scared in her life. She was feeling confused. How can this be, John and I have both talked to him. Finally, at the house she got to the kitchen, she collapsed on the chair nearest to the door. She couldn't believe what happened. She thought, what will I do. She's moving through the kitchen talking to herself. I need to stay calm, I need to think. Think Charlotte, damn it, think. Then she came up with an idea. I need to find out when Joe died. When I find out that much, I'll know when Sarah died too. So if what Jessie says is true, the transition should take place at that time. Then it dawned on her, that she may be able to find out something from Mrs. Darcy. The first thing she needed to know was the exact date of the Captains death. That will give her an approximate date to Sarah's appearance and with that in mind she headed for the front door and grabbed her car keys on the way out. She drove as fast as she dared to straight to Mrs. Darcy's house. She felt the urgent need to find out as much as she could as soon as possible. Finally she pulled into the driveway and went to the entrance way of the house. When she stopped the car she got out so fast she left the door hanging wide open. She rang the doorbell and beat on it impatiently. Saying to herself, Please be home, Oh please be here. Finally the door swung open. Mrs. Darcy wasn't surprised in the least to see Charlotte.

She ask Charlotte to come in and Charlotte right away said, we need to talk. There's something going on out there and the old man said they need me to help. I can't help if I don't know what's happening. Mrs. Darcy said, calm yourself child and I'll try to help. Please follow me. Mrs. Darcy led Charlotte to her study. She ask Charlotte to reach up on the top shelf of her bookcase and hand down the two books she pointed to. Charlotte handed her the books and Mrs. Darcy took them and sat down. She slowly rubbed her hands over the books to dust them off and she looked up at Charlotte and said, You know that once you start this thing you can't turn back. Charlotte was getting angry. She was tired of all the garbage and wanted to get to the point. She then said to Mrs. Darcy. Start what? What in the hell are you talking about. What's going on out there? You know, I know you do. So start talking. Mrs. Darcy said, please Charlotte calm yourself, I can't talk to you like this. If you calm down I'll explain. But when I tell you, you might not believe me any way. So I have to ask you to listen carefully.

Charlotte was trying to calm herself but it was very difficult. Mrs. Darcy knew when she sold them the place that something was wrong there. Charlotte was thinking it was unfair for her to let them take their children into a place that may be harmful to them. But at this point in time, she didn't even think about what she had said to John, when they were looking at the house. She said, she wanted it no matter what. Well now she has it and doesn't know what to do about it. Charlotte was calming down a little and Mrs. Darcy saw that she could talk to her now a little easier. She said, My dear may I ask if you believe in the here after? Charlotte said, what do you mean by the hereafter. Yes! I believe there is something after death, but I don't know what. Mrs. Darcy then said, well do you believe in the Super Natural? Charlotte said yes, I think I do and Mrs. Darcy said, good that will make things a little easier to explain. Mrs. Darcy said, Charlotte listen carefully. What's happening out there is of the Super Natural and when dealing with such, you have to be extremely careful and most important of all is once you start there's no turning back. There's so much energy out there and it's mostly Negative energy. The Spirits are very angry, they want to be together, but so many years have gone by and the truth about their deaths have never been revealed. So you see Child! They were cheated from life and now their being tormented in death. I've known about this since I was a little girl. I suspected something when I went to the house one day. I went there out of curiosity and I wanted to look around. I was there quite awhile and finally I went behind the house.

There I ran face to face with an old man. Needless to say, he scared the daylights out of me, but when he spoke to me, I knew instantly that he wasn't there to harm me. He introduced himself to me and told me he was my Great Uncle Jessie. Well that was a little hard for me to swallow. My Great Uncle died many years ago. So, I thought this man was either playing with my mind or I was talking to a ghost. We talked awhile and the more he talked about the family the more I realized that he was in the family. He knew things that only family could know. Then, I knew for sure, I was talking to the ghost of my Great Uncle. So you see Charlotte, things happen and we really don't understand why they do, but they do. You see while I spoke to my Great Uncle's ghost. He told me how he died and I know it to be true because the family told the exact same story. Only they didn't tell it in the detail he told it in. He told me exactly what happened on that day even down to the pain and agony he felt at his death. It must be a horrible way to die with flames all around and nowhere to go. Well anyway! Let me tell you about my Great Uncle Jessie. Jessie died in the old place that belonged to my Great Grandparents. Everyone except Jessie went to church one Sunday morning. He wasn't feeling well so he stayed home and in bed. They never really knew what happened or how the fire started. It was all a big mystery. There was no reason for the house to burn so they looked around and out behind the woodshed they found oil for the lamps spilled all over the ground. By all the evidence they found, they came to the conclusion the fire had been set, but they never knew who or why.

But! unfortunately, Jessie died in that fire. They found his body along side the body of another man. No one knew who the other man was. Jessie was at the house alone and in the ruins they found a sack filled with jewelry and other valuables that were apparently being stolen. So they figured the house was being robbed and the burglar set the fire.

Mrs. Darcy took a short breather before she continued her story. Charlotte was quite interested in what she was hearing and took in every small detail. Mrs. Darcy began again and told Charlotte about the day she came in contact with the ghost of Jessie and how he told the truth of his death. Mrs. Darcy began again by telling Charlotte about Jessie's death. She said he told her that the day he died was a most horrible experience. She told the story just as Jessie told her years ago. I was asleep in my bedroom when I awoke suddenly to the smell of smoke. I panicked and jumped out of bed. I knew there was no one else in the house, so I tried to run to the stairway. Flames had already swallowed the steps and the only way out was down the servants steps which led to the kitchen. The smoke was heavy and I could hardly see my way down the steps.

Finally I got to the bottom and felt my way to the back door. I was almost there when I heard something behind me. I turned to see what it was and in the smoke there was a man standing there. He tried to hit me with a thick board and I ducked and at that point I realized, he was the man who started the blaze. He was there for no good and he needed me to die in the fire so I wouldn't be able to tell who started the fire. He lunged at me again and we fell to the floor. The smoke was so thick it was burning my eyes. The man hit me hard across my head and I fell into the flames. I wasn't going to die and let this man live, so I held on as tight as I could and drug him into the flames with me. The last thing I remember about my death was the agonizing pain, but as I took my last breath I felt great peace in knowing that the man who took my life would die too. Mrs. Darcy looked at Charlotte and said, You see dear, Jessie avenged his own death, but it was to late for him to cross over to the here after. So, now his soul wanders until he can find a way to cross over and the only way for him to do that, is to try to find peace for the Captain and his loved one. Jessie comes and goes at will, because his spirit is free and at peace, so he works both sides of the wall of energy. He truly want to help the young spirits to become free.

Charlotte said, OK! I understand all that, but what's that got to do with me? Mrs. Darcy looked down at the books she was holding. She didn't know how to say what needed to be said. She slowly moved her eyes up to meet Charlotte's and said, Sarah needs your body and strength. If she had your physical form, she could break down the wall of energy and cross over to the Captain. In two weeks come Saturday, is the anniversary date of the Captain's death and the time between now and then. Will become very difficult. Sarah will be making her presence known. If you really believe and want to help their tortured souls you have to open yourself to her. Let her enter your body peacefully. She'll slip right in and when it's all over you'll be fine. I swear to you, that she won't harm you. She only needs to use your body and strength to get to where she has to go. But remember! If you do decide to help them. No one and I mean no one, can interfere. If they do, it could destroy you. By this time, Charlotte's head was spinning. She said, this is the craziest thing I've ever heard. Why me? Of all the people in this world. Why does Sarah need me? There must be someone else who can help. Mrs. Darcy said, "Quite Harshly" No! Your missing the whole point. You my dear, are the direct decedent of Sarah. That makes your chemistry the same as hers. You are blood of her blood and flesh of her flesh. That's the reason your body is susceptible to hers. Your body will except Sarah's spirit openly, if you have a mind to, and of course! If there's no outside interference.

Charlotte said, God! I can't believe what I'm hearing. She turned and headed for the door and on her way she said, this is all to much for me. I have to get out of here. I need time to think. I have to go. Mrs. Darcy ran after her and said, but Charlotte you have no time. It's your destination, you are the one who was chosen. It's been handed down through the generations. "YOU ARE THE ONE!" When you talked about the music. I knew it was you. The tune was Sarah's favorite tune and Joe had it played for her the night they announced their engagement. When you first heard it, you thought it was beautiful and John thought it was weird. You excepted it as Sarah once did. She was enchanted by it and now you are too. So you see Charlotte, It's started already and the music is the beginning. Charlotte was standing by the door. She said to Mrs. Darcy, Ok! If that's the beginning, what's next? Mrs. Darcy looked straight into Charlotte's eyes and said, I don't know. No one knows what fate has in store for you. But! It is truely your destination. Charlotte opened the door and went outside. Mrs. Darcy followed her. She reached out to Charlotte and took her by the hand. Charlotte turned to look at Mrs. Darcy and she was speechless. Mrs. Darcy squeezed her hand and said, God be with you and keep you safe. But remember, when Sarah comes to you.

Except her openly, she won't hurt you Charlotte, I swear. She needs you. Charlotte never spoke a word, she just walked to the car. Her head is spinning. She's thinking she has entered into a bad dream and can't wake up. Her hearts pounding and she's scared to death. She doesn't know what's going to happen or when. She starts the car and heads for home. All the way home, she thought of nothing else. She needed to find a way to tell John or maybe she won't tell him and let it happen. But that wouldn't be fair to him. Then she found herself wandering when it'll happen and how will she know for sure, when it does. She pulled into the driveway and as she did she thought about the date of the Captain's death. All she knows is that in two weeks it's going to take place. But, no one's sure of the date of Sarah's death. They only know that two or three days after the Captain died, Sarah disappeared. So, Charlotte decided to go straight to the tomb to read the dates on it. She remembered that she and John never did clear all the weeds away to read the inscription. She ran all the way through the old Cemetery. When she got to the old willow tree, she stopped to rest. She looked up at the tomb and felt instant fear. She was scared to death of being there but she had to know. The fear got the best of her and she started to tremble. She was shaking so bad her knees buckled under and she fell to the ground. She sat there and cried like a baby.

After she cried most of her fear away she was feeling confused as she sat and quietly wept. The afternoon passed slowly, as she sat on the ground staring at the tomb. She's lost in time. The trees are flowing lazily in the cool autumn air, but Charlotte feels nothing. Then finally she comes back to reality. She looked at the tomb and remembered why she was there. The dates, I need the dates. When she got to her feet she turned towards the tomb. She slowly raise her head to look at the entrance and right before her eyes the Captain appeared. Charlotte was petrified. She tried to move her legs, but they wouldn't move. It was like an unseen force was holding them. She tried to move her head and again couldn't move. It was like the Captain was controlling her body. He didn't come any closer, he just stood and stared into Charlotte's eyes. Charlotte had no choice but to stare back at him and as she watched him, he began to move. His transparent form slowly paced in front of the tomb. He then turned back to Charlotte and tried to speak. His mouth was moving but no words would come. But Charlotte knew somehow, what he was saying. In his eyes she saw the pain and agony he was feeling and knew the torment he felt in his heart. It wasn't hard to figure out that he was saying, "PLEASE HELP PLEASE."

After those words were finished being formed on his lips, he turned into a fine mist and completely vanished. Charlotte tried to move again and this time nothing was stopping her. She turned away as fast as she could and ran to the house. Once she got there she went in and locked all the windows and doors. She was terrified. She had been told what was going to happen but she couldn't bring herself to deal with it. She had to calm herself and think. Charlotte went to the kitchen, she needed a strong cup of coffee. She didn't smoke but she needed to now. John's friend left a pack cigarettes there when they were working and Charlotte took one from the pack. She lit it and took a long drag off of it. She nearly killed herself from choking on it and after she finished coughing she put it out and settled for her coffee. She sat down at the table with her cup in her hand. She thought real hard about what Mrs. Darcy told her. Then she realized that the only way she could deal with this, was to let fate run it's course. If she was the one chosen, then there was no place to run. Charlotte made herself busy. She needed to keep her mind occupied. The children would be home from school soon and she had to get supper started. She was trying to figure out what to tell John while she was cooking. She had know idea how he was going to react to the news. So, she decided to wait until later to break it to him. Maybe even wait until the children were in bed. After she decided to wait until later, she made herself busy in the kitchen.

But it seems that know matter how busy she was, she could think of nothing else. She kept thinking of Sarah and the Captain and was feeling great sympathy for the young lovers. She realizes they have been dead for over a century. But if the stories are true, their still suffering. Their souls have been in constent torment since their deaths. But, how do you know what to believe? As far as Charlotte's concerned she has to see to believe and she a little skeptical about the whole thing. She stops and looks around the house and wonders what truth is hidden in those old walls. Then she thinks, when will I know, or how? "If ever."

Chapter Nine

SARAH COME'S THROUGH

The School Bus dropped the children off at the end of the lane. Charlotte went out to meet them. On the way to the house the children were running and playing on their way down the lane. They got down to the well when Charlotte noticed there was still roses blooming in the rose garden. She went to pick a rose and immediately pricked her finger on a big thorn. She was bleeding, but didn't notice how much she bled. The blood ran down her finger and on to the soil and as it hit the dirt it absorbed instantly and the ground took on a blueish green glow. Charlotte didn't notice the glow as she went on to pick her flowers. She decided to clean up the garden and pull weeds away from her bushes.

The leaves that were dropping from the trees were laying heavy around the bushes. When she was almost finished she stood back and admired the roses. She thought how beautiful the garden was laid out and the location was perfect. She was ready to turn and walk to the house when she noticed a rose in the back part of the garden. She couldn't believe her eyes. It looked like a black rose and it was one of the most beautiful flowers she has ever seen. Charlotte walked back towards the rose to get a better look. She reached out her hand to touch it and the music began to play. The Mandolins played and she was completely mesmerized by the sound. Reality seemed to slowly slip away as the music played and Charlotte heard nothing but The melody of The Sweethearts Waltz. At that point she seemed to be lost somewhere in time.

"The music was the beginning. From this time on, Sarah will become stronger. The blood in the soil helped to strengthen her spirit. It was enough nourishment for her to start the transition. Now! For Charlotte there's no turning back and from now on, things will only get harder". Charlotte was brought back to reality by the children. They were terrorized and screaming at her from the well. She shook her head to clear it and ran to see what was wrong. When she got to them she tried to touch them to calm them and they pulled away.

They were scared to death and it was Charlotte, that they were afraid of. She didn't understand what was happening. She said to them, what's wrong with you? It's me! It's Mommy! The boy said, "with his voice shaking". How did you do that? Charlotte said, what? How did I do what? The boy said, How did you change to look like someone else? It was you, I know it was, but you looked like another woman. How did you do it? Charlotte didn't know what to say. How do you explain when you don't know yourself what's happening. So she did the next best thing, she lied to them. She tried to tell them that she was magic and then made a joke of it. She said, I was playing a trick on you. It didn't work very well but the children were a little calmer now. Probably because their mother was back to normal and talking to them. At this point, they headed back to the house. On their way, both the children kept their distance from her. Every time Charlotte looked at one of them, they were staring at her. It made her very uncomfortable, but then she realized that the children shouldn't be there when this thing took place. She thought, My God! their terrified already and It's me that their afraid of and Charlotte realized that it could be very dangerous for them to stay. So, she had to find a way to get them away from here. Charlotte went in the house and straight to the telephone. She called her mom and talked to her for awhile. She started out with just ordinary conversation, but her Mom knowing her very well, knew that something was very wrong. Her mother ask, Charlotte are you alright? Charlotte said, actually no, I'm not alright. Could you come over so we can talk. Her Mother said, hang on honey, I'll be right there.

Her mom dropped everything she was doing and went straight to Charlotte's house. She knew in her heart that her daughter needed her. When she got there, Charlotte looked terrible. Her complexion was pale and chalky looking and her eyes were sunken and blood shot. She looked as though she was totally exhausted. Her mother went over to her and ask if she was sick. All Charlotte said to her mom was, we need to talk. Charlotte looked at the floor all the time she spoke to her mother. Their eyes never met as they went to the kitchen to get coffee and sit down at the table.

Charlotte got the coffee ready while her mom sat impatiently waiting for an explanation. She was very anxious to find out why Charlotte needed her. Meanwhile, Charlotte checked on the children to make sure they couldn't over hear their conversation. She was relieved to find them in the back yard playing on the tire swing. Now, she felt it was safe to talk to her mother without any interruptions. Charlotte sat the coffee on the table in front of her mom and put hers down in front of her. She sat down and stared at the cup. She picked up her spoon and fumbled with it, she was extremely nervous. So her mother sat quietly until Charlotte was ready to talk.

She didn't want to rush her because she knew her daughter very well and know something was really wrong. She also knew what ever it was, it was something Charlotte couldn't handle alone and had no other choice but to ask for help. Charlotte finally spoke. She said, Mom, I'm so scared. You were right, all the stories that you heard, well there is some truth to them. She slowly raised her head and looked into her mother's eyes. She said, can you help me? I need you to take the children home with you for a short time. Charlotte's mother reached across the table and took Charlotte by the hand and said, Honey I'll do what ever you need me to do but "Please" tell me what's wrong. Charlotte looked away from her mother's stare and said, OK! I'll tell you. Charlotte said, Mom, it all started at your house. Do you remember the day I was at your house and we were in the attic and I fell to the floor? Her mother nodded and Charlotte continued. Well, I felt something and it was really weird. I felt this strange tingle all through my body and pretty soon I started to see these flashes. They reminded me of a slide projector showing pictures only I was the only one who could see them. In the flashes was a man, a very angry man. He was hitting something and it looked like he was yelling at something or someone. I couldn't see, but I really think it was another person he was yelling at and then I woke up on the floor.

I'm not sure what happened that day but I know that it was the beginning. The women from that point on talked the whole afternoon. Charlotte opened herself and told her mother everything that's been happening ever since. Even all the things Mrs. Darcy had told her. When Charlotte finished talking to her mom. Her mother sat quietly and just stared at her coffee cup. All the things she just heard was racing around in her head. She was feeling fear for her daughter's life and the safty of her family. But, she knew if she said anything about it, it would only be a waste of time. But she did say, Honey, you know you can leave this place and maybe then it will all come to an end for you. Charlotte stood up and walked over to the sink. She stood there staring out the window looking out over the meadow. She turned and said, but Mom, you don't understand. I can't run, something inside of me is eating me up. I have to stay and finished this thing. Please try to understand. Sarah needs me and I have to try to help her. We need to find out the truth. Charlotte's Mom sat quietly and looked at Charlotte. She couldn't help but think that something like this could be extremely dangerous. And even though she doesn't quite understand what's been happening, she is very concerned about the safety and well being of her daughter. But then on the other hand, she respects her daughter's feelings. She also knows that whatever she might say or do, will not change her daughters mind, once it's been made up.

And at that very moment she was feeling great pride for her daughter. Now the women came to the point of conversation about the children. Like what clothes they'll need for school, what time they have to catch the bus, what time school starts and lets out and important information about each child. Charlotte wasn't really happy about all of this because she's never been away from the children before. Maybe for a night when they went to sleep at a friends house but not for very long. She was certainly going to miss them but she knew it was in their best interest. So the women got everything ready and all they had to do now was wait for John to come home and tell him about what's going on.

Charlotte looked at the clock in the bedroom, they were so busy packing close she didn't start supper yet. She said, come on Mom. We have to get to the kitchen and start cooking. John will be home soon and there's nothing ready. So, Charlotte and her Mother went to the kitchen to fix supper. Charlotte put steaks on the broiler and her Mom peeled potatoes. While they were busy they talked about the house. Everything in it was so beautiful, but there was a coldness about it. When you walked from room to room you could feel the change. The house most definitely had cold spots, which made it uncomfortable at times. By now, supper was almost finished. The conversation went on the whole time.

Then all of a sudden Charlotte slumped over the sink. She was in extreme pain, she grabbed her head and was holding her eyes closed. Her Mom dropped the dinner plates and ran to her. She said; Honey are you OK? But,Charlotte didn't answer her. She stared at her mom like she didn't even know her. Then her mom said; Charlotte what's wrong with you? Charlotte began to speak. She spoke in a very low and delicate voice and the words came slow and were drawn. She said, Why Ma'am Who's Charlotte? My name is Sarah! Who might you be? Charlotte's mother was shocked. She backed away from her daughter and stared at her. Neither of them spoke another word. They both stood in disbelief and stared at each other. To Sarah the woman looked very strange in her clothing and Sarah of course didn't recognize her. She was Charlotte's mother, not Sarah's. Suddenly, Sarah began to shake her head violently. She stopped and looked at Charlotte's mom. She spoke again and this time it was the voice of Charlotte. She said to her mother, Mom what's wrong are you och? She saw the fear on her mother's face and knew something happened, but didn't have the slightest idea what. Her Mom said, Honey is that you? Charlotte said, of course it's me and her mom ran to her and hugged her. She told Charlotte that it has begun. Sarah is coming through. Charlotte looked at her mom with a puzzled look on her face and said, how do you know? And her Mother told her what had just taken place. Charlotte was devastated, her mind was racing as she paced the floor.

Finally she said, this can't be. This is awful, does this mean I won't know what's happening or even remember? How will I know John and the kids and how will I know about them? This must mean that Sarah will take over completely. What if she likes being me? What will happen to me if she decides to stay? Charlotte stopped pacing. She said to her mother. Mom I don't know if I can handle this and what about John. How will he deal with me becoming a total stranger? Charlotte is very upset by all of this, she begins to pace again. Charlotte's mom tries to lighten the mood a little. She said jokingly. Maybe John will like the idea of you becoming another woman. It's not everyday a man gets to sleep with two women and if he wants something strange all he has to do is go to bed and there he'll find his strange stuff. Charlotte was shocked by what her mother just said. She said, Mother! How can you joke at a time like this? This is serious. Maybe John won't like it and what if he can't deal with it either. Maybe he'll leave me. Then what? At this point, Charlotte was extremely upset. Now she had to worry about how she was going to break the news to John because he just pulled into the driveway. But on the other hand, John was parking the car and was delighted to see Charlotte's mom was there. He liked her very much and was always happy to see her.

He got out of the car and went over to say hello to the children and went into the house. He laid some papers on the table in the entrance hall and went to the kitchen and as soon as he walked through the door, his mood changed. He saw Charlotte and her mother and knew instantly, that something was wrong. John walked over to Charlotte. She was trembling and he ask if she was alright. Charlotte looked up and said to him, Yes and no, we need to talk. John looked at Charlotte's mother and then back to Charlotte. He said, now's as good a time as any and went to the table to sit down. When he got comfortable Charlotte started at the beginning and told John everything. She told him about the first time they were in the house and she saw Sarah in the mirror. Then she continued until she told him everything that has happened until now. John sat at the table quietly. When he finally spoke he was angry. He stood up and told Charlotte to start packing. He said; I won't live in this place when your in danger. It could also be dangerous for the kids. Charlotte said, the kids will be alright. They won't be here. I,m sending them with Mom for a couple of weeks and if Mrs. Darcy is right, in two weeks come Saturday, it'll all be over. "John was really angry now". He said, what in the hell are you saying. Are you telling me that you intend to stay and go through with this? Charlotte looked at John with a very positive look and said; Yes I do. John said, but why? Why on earth would you want to go through with this? It could be dangerous, you could get hurt or - or even worse. He dropped his head and said, God! I don't even want to think about what could happen. He raised his head and looked straight into Charlotte's eyes and said, "We're Not Staying"... Charlotte stood quietly and took in John's every word, but now was the time, for her to stand her ground. She said; if you don't want to stay, that's fine. But! I'm not leaving. There's something inside me that's telling me, I have to do this and I am going to see this thing through, with or without you. So, no matter what happens, I have to help these poor lost souls or at least try. "John was furious". He stormed out of the kitchen and went out to the porch. He needed some time to cool off before he really lost control of his temper. He stayed outside most of the evening and thought about all the things Charlotte had talked about. He remembered the night the old man was peeking in the window and the more he thought about all that was happening, the more he felt uneasy about the whole situation. It was all beginning to become quite eerie. Then John remembered the Captain and thought about how he felt when the Captain materialized right in front of them. The look on his face as he floated to the edge of the Cemetery and then John realized the wall of energy must run right through there. The Captain came as close as he dared to and at that point, John realized there must be some truth to all this, after all.

Finally after all the time John had to think, he went back into the house. He felt a little better about the whole thing. He went to the kitchen were the women were and said to Charlotte. Are you sure about all this? Charlotte said, I've never been so sure about anything in my entire life. And John said; you'll be safe, right? Charlotte said;

if you have enough faith and believe strong enough, everthing will work out. So, with that in mind, I believe, I can do this. John walked over and hugged Charlotte. He turned to Charlotte's Mother and said; I appreciate all your help and taking care of the children for us. Hopefully, it'll be over soon. The evening went a lot smoother from that time on. Charlotte's mother spent the evening with the family. Her husband was on a job and wouldn't be home until late, so she had time to spend with them. After the kitchen was cleaned up from supper they all went to the living room to watch television. They enjoyed their visit and around eight o'clock Charlotte's mom said she had better be running along. She said; I have two youngsters to get ready for bed and I'm a little out of practice. John laughed and said; don't worry Ema, they'll tell you what to do and they all laughed. The women left the room to get things ready to go. When they got everything ready, John and Charlotte walked them to the door. They kissed and hugged the children and told them to be good for their grandmother. Charlotte then hugged her mother and thanked her for being so understanding.

Charlotte whispered in her ear, not to worry and that she would keep her informed as things happened. Her mom said; I love you honey, Please be careful and she got to the car and waved as she drove away. John put his arm around Charlotte and they stood quietly as they watched Ema drive away with the children. They both had their own thoughts, but kept them quiet for the present time. John turned to go into the house and grabbed Charlotte by the hand. He led her in the house and straight to the kitchen. He said he was a little hungry and they made a snack and as they were eating they enjoyed each others company. Soon the conversation turned to the matters at hand. As they discussed the situation, they decided not to worry about it and take things as they come. At this point, all they could do was wait and let everything run it's course.

Chapter Ten

THE WALL OF ENERGY

The next couple of days went without incident. John was beginning to believe it was all a hoax of some kind. And he was believing the laugh was on them, because they were the center of it. Soon a week has come and gone and still nothing has happened. Charlotte told John they had to hang in there for eight more days. If nothing happened within the eight days then nothing ever will and they're conversation turned to the children.

Charlotte told John that the house was so empty without the kids. They both missed the bickering and running through the rooms. Their laughter seemed to keep the house alive. But they both knew it was for the best and decided to make the best of it. They went to the living room to watch television for awhile. They cuddled on the sofa and decided to turn in early. Charlotte went to take her bath and John told her he would meet her in the bedroom. He was feeling pretty passionate by the time Charlotte got there. When Charlotte finished she went to the bedroom. She got under the covers and John attacked her. She was laughing so hard she had tears in her eyes. Finally they got serious, they were necking and fooling around under the covers. Soon they were at the point of passion and making wild passionate love. They were both feeling great pleasure.

"When all of a sudden". Charlotte started screaming and hitting John. She was crying hysterically. John stopped and tried to
comfort her and that only made things worse. She fought him even
more. John finally rolled off of Charlotte and laid on the bed beside
her. Charlotte immediately jumped out of bed and ran to the corner
where the dressing table sat. She slouched down in fetal position with
her head on her knees and cried her heart out. John was feeling great
sympathy for her, although he had no idea what was happening. He
was a little scared of the way she was acting. He was beginning to
think he did something wrong. He went over to her and helped her
to her feet and held her in his arms. At this point she didn't fight him
any longer and John became very confused, but not for long. As he
held Charlotte in his arms, he looked into the mirror of the dressing
table and then and only then, did he understand what had happened.

Charlotte wasn't Charlotte at all, she som how became Sarah and
the woman looking back at him was a very beautiful but unhappy
woman. John was totally stunned. He couldn't believe his eyes. He
pulled away from Charlotte and looked into her face. He was looking at his wife but when he looked back at the mirror, he saw Sarah
again. John tried real hard not to lose control. He just stood there
and held Charlotte until she calmed down. When she finally got
control of herself she slowly backed away from John. She never took
her eyes off of him as she backed all the way across the room to the
double doors that led out to the balcony.

When she got to them she stopped. She turned and started to
open the doors but for some reason she changed her mind. She turned
back around and said to John. Your a kind and gentle man, but you
must leave here at once. Joe wouldn't take to kindly to a strange
man being in my quarters and it would make him very unhappy to
know your here. So, please leave. And this time she turn and opened
the doors. John was speechless as he watched her go out on the balcony. He ran to the door to make sure Sarah didn't hurt Charlotte.
When he got to the doors he stopped dead in his tracks. The sight
he saw was unbelievable. The night was very dark and the sky was
crystal clear. Charlotte was standing with her hands on the railing.
The wind was blowing through her hair and she was beautiful in the

moonlight. She was looking towards the Cemetery. Then John knew what Charlotte had told him about, because then was the first time John had laid eyes on the wall of energy. He was astonished. The wall of energy was a fantastic sight and you had to see it to believe it. It was like the energy ran in waves, the constant flow ran all the way around the house. It became a bubble of energy and as the energy flowed around the house there was a blueish green glow coming from it. Outside of the bubble was a heavy mist laying all around the grounds. John looked out through it and saw the apparition of the Captain and the old man.

They stood waiting patiently for Sarah. John walked over to Charlotte and stood beside her. He looked into her face and in the moonlight he saw the twinkle of a tear on her cheek. Then came another and then another. John realized he was watching his wife longing for another man and was soon to realize he was being foolish. The woman was his wife only in physical form, for in spirit she was Sarah and she's waited an eternity for her young lover. He simply stood by and watched as he saw the yearning in her eyes. She extended her arms towards the cemetery and the Captain returned the gesture and Charlotte collapsed. She hit the floor hard and John knelt beside her to see if she was ok. Charlotte looked up at him and raised her hand to him, as she did their eyes met and John knew instantly that his Charlotte was back. Charlotte tried to get up but the pain in her head was to great. She put her hands on her head and said, the pain is unbearable. Then she knew something had happened. The last thing she remembered was they were in bed making love and now she finds herself outside on the balcony floor with a severe headache. Charlotte looked up at John and said, honey what happened? He said, come on let me help you back to bed and then I'll try to explain. He helped Charlotte to her feet and she collapsed again.

She was to weak from her ordeal to walk, so John carried her. He laid her on the bed and Charlotte immediately wanted to know what happened. John looked at Charlotte, he wasn't quite sure how to tell her everything that took place. So he simply started at the beginning and told her everything. Charlotte couldn't believe her ears. She said; your telling me, you actually saw the wall of energy?

John said, Yes I did and it was the most fascinating thing I've ever seen in my life. Charlotte sat quietly for a minute and said, so what your saying is that it's true? John said; yeah, I guess it is. It sure made a believer out of me.

Charlotte still couldn't believe what all happened. She said, John tell me again what all took place and be sure not to leave anything out. So, John started at the beginning again and was careful not to leave out even the smallest of details. When he finished, Charlotte looked sad. John said; honey what's wrong? She said; you actually saw the two of them, right? John said; yes I did. Why? She said; they're really unhappy aren't they? John said; yeah, with sadness in his voice and said; my heart ached for both of them. They were both being tormented needlessly and now I see why it's so important for you to help them. They're suffering more than any being should and I can see now why they need you. Your the one who'll put an end to their suffering.

After they talked awhile, Charlotte finally said, I'm exhausted. They went to bed and went right to sleep. Both of them slept quietly. For the remainder of the night, was a peaceful one. John woke early, he got up before his alarm went off. He went to get a shower and in awhile Charlotte came in. She said; good morning. Did you sleep well last night? John peeked out of the shower and said; like a baby. How about you? Charlotte said; I had the best sleep of my life. I didn't dream or move a muscle all night. John said; great, after what you went through last night, you deserved to get a good night's sleep. John ask Charlotte to hand him his towel. He wrapped it around him and got out of the shower. As he was drying his hair he told Charlotte, he was thinking about calling off work for the day and spend it at home with her. Charlotte said; great, I could sure use the company today. Then John said; I have an even better idea. The Company owes me quite a few weeks vacation. So, how about I call and ask for a couple of weeks off. Then by the time I have to go back, this might be all over with and we can get back to our normal lives.

Charlotte was quiet. John said; Honey is something wrong? She said; No, I just feel bad about you having to miss work. She said; remember, we planned on you taking your vacation in the spring.

John said; Honey you worry to much and besides I really don't want to have to worry about you being alone here while I'm at work. And just think, we can get a lot of work done around here while I'm off. So they agreed. John takes vacation.

Charlotte went to the kitchen to start breakfast. John came in while the eggs were frying. They sat down to eat and decided to work outside today. The yard was filled with leaves and the rose gardens needed cleaned. After they finished their breakfast, they headed outside. They went to the woodshed to man themselves with the tools they needed for their job. The first thing they were going to do was rake all the leaves. It was a hugh lawn, so it would take awhile to get them all piled up to burn. They worked on it for a couple of hours and finally they were all ready for the match. John said to Charlotte, let me have the honor of lighting up your life today, My Dearest Lady.

Meanwhile Charlotte is dancing with the rake. They were enjoying the work and making the best of it. It seemed to go much quicker if they got pleasure from it. They were playing in the leaves and rolling around like the children do when they help. John was chasing Charlotte and she ran behind the tree. John caught her and they fell to the ground, they were laughing so hard they lost all track of time. After they gained control of themselves. They decided to get busy and get their work done. John started the leaves to burning and headed to the garage to get the tractor. He wanted to cut the grass one last time before the snow flies. Charlotte finished putting all the leaves on the fire and went to the Rose garden to clean it up. Charlotte loves her roses and tends to them all the time. The roses were still blooming and were beautiful. Up until this time the weather has been very mild and they have had very little frost, so the roses were thriving beautifully. Charlotte had her trimmers in her hand and started to nip all the dead stems away. John at this time was almost finished with the lawn. All he had to do now, was cut around the well. John saw Charlotte in the garden, he stopped the tractor and went to help her clean up some of the debre.

When he got to the garden he loaded his arms with rubbish and took it to the fire to burn. Charlotte was so busy, she didn't see John at all. After John put the dab re on the fire, he walked back towards the garden. He look at Charlotte and watched her, he noticed she was acting strange. He stopped and stood very still while he watched her. Charlotte was on her knees, she was doubled over. John knew that something was wrong and went towards her. As he got closer he heard her crying. John then ran to her and when he got to Charlotte he knelt on the ground beside her. He said, Honey what's wrong? She looked at him and threw her arms around his neck. She cried so hard she was trembling. Finally after a short time she was calm enough to tell John why she was crying.

Charlotte sat staring at the roses. Her face was swollen and her eyes were red from crying. She was terrified for some reason and John needed to know why. He said to her, Honey talk to me and Charlotte proceeded to tell John what happened. She told him she had the flashes again, only this time they frightened me terribly. John reached down and pulled Charlotte to her feet. He led her back to the well so she could sit down on the bench. When she sat down she told John that in her flashes she saw Sarah. She said she saw Sarah down by the river and she was alone. She was sitting at the edge of the water and she was crying. It must have been the time she learned of the Captain's death. After she sat awhile she turned to go back to her carriage and turned face to face with that ugly, dirty man. This man must be the one she wrote about in her diary. She tried to go around the man and he reached out and grabbed her. He held her so tight that he hurt her arms. She tried to pull away and he hurt her more. She began to struggle and fight with the man, but it was no use. The more she fought the madder he got and finally he got so mad, he started to beat her. She fought harder and the more she fought, the harder he hit her. The man was insane and he hit her again and again. Sarah fought with all her might, but it was no use. He was much stronger than Sarah and she collapsed. She fell to the ground and the man drug her to the weeds.

When he got her out of sight of the road, he threw her to the ground and started to rip off all of her clothes. Sarah screamed and all the man did was laugh at her. She kicked him in the crouch area and tried to get away. He grabbed her dress and pulled her back to the ground. When she fell, she hit her head on an old tree stump.

The man jumped on top of her and punched her as hard as he could. Sarah never moved after that. The man was not concerned about Sarah, he thought she only passed out so he continued to do what he wanted. He raped the poor helpless girl, again and again. But soon he noticed she wasn't breathing. He then realized he had murdered her. He paniced and tried to figure out how to hide the body. He couldn't throw her in the river. She was all bruised and if they found her they would know that someone beat her up. So he sat and tried to think. Finally he remembered, that at the girls house, they were still working on the grounds. There he was sure to find a place to bury her. He grabbed the girls arms and drug her to his horse. He struggled to get the body up over the horse and finally he managed. Her limp body hung over the saddle on both sides. Blood ran down the stirrups to the ground. When the man saw the blood he panicked even more. He then ran to Sarah's carriage and hit the horse's. He tried to run them away, but they only made a circle and came right back to the place where Sarah tied them. After he ran the horse's off, he mounted his horse and quickly rode off to find a place to bury the girl.

Charlotte sat quietly for awhile. John sat and waited patiently for her to begin to speak again. She didn't say a word, but John had to know more. He needed to understand what Charlotte was seeing. He said to her. Charlotte, talk to me. Honey, are you telling me, that you saw in the flashes the man that killed Sarah? Charlotte said, Yes I think so, I even watched him rape her repeatedly and beat her unmercifully. John, I don't understand what's happening. It's been some time now since I've had those flashes. Why now? What made them start again? It seems like something has triggered them. Is it Sarah herself that's trying to tell me something? John said; I don't know honey, but maybe Mrs. Darcy was right, when she said that there was a truth to be found. Charlotte was exhausted after her ordeal. John said to her, let's call it a day. She agreed and they went to the house to get cleaned up, so they could go and see the children. They really needed some time away from the house. Charlotte was looking a little peaked these days and needed some time to relax. The strain has been tremendous for her. So they went to spend some quality time with her parents and the children. It took them about an hour to get ready to go. Charlotte called ahead to make sure they would be home and everything was all set. John and Charlotte got there just in time for supper. They ate and after the kitchen was cleaned up, they went to the living room to sit and relax while they were visiting.

Most all of their conversation was about all the things that have been happening. Ema agrees with John, she too, thinks that Sarah is coming through and is trying to tell Charlotte something. She told Charlotte to be extra careful and don't take any unnecessary chances. Meanwhile, Charlotte's father is sitting quietly and taking in the whole conversation. When Charlotte was finished he looked at John with a very stern face and said; If that was my wife, I would put my foot down and get her the hell out of that place. If she didn't want to go then I'd drag her if I had to. He said; John what are you waiting for? Do you want something terrible to happen to her? What the hell's the matter with you man?

Charlotte's father caught John completely off guard. John didn't expect an outburst like that from him, but he quickly reacted. He said, Please sir, I'm sorry your so upset, but please believe me when I tell you I've tried to get her out, but she won't budge. She said she was staying even if it meant staying there by herself and besides that, you know her as well as I do and she'd only go back even if I did. Her Dad looked at John with a pleading look on his face. He knew he was out of line and now it's time to face the truth. He said to John, I'm sorry I snapped at you and your right. She has been head strong since she was a baby and no one can change her mind. Once it's been made up and about that time, Charlotte broke up the conversation and asked John if he was ready to go home. Charlotte and John went to see the children before they left. They were all tucked in for the night and they kissed them both and headed for home. It was around ten o'clock when they reached the driveway. John turned the car in and went up the lane. When they reached the top of the knoll, he stopped the car. Charlotte gasped, she looked through the windshield and was completely astonished at the spectacular sight that was before them. She said to John, "My God, What is that?" John took her by the hand and said, Remember last night when I told you about the energy? Well there it is, now you see it for yourself. Charlotte was amazed at the sight. She said, but look at it. It's all around the house and seems to get thicker and heavier at the Cementer. John said, yeah, just look at it. You know, I just realized that, that might be the reason the house has been so well preserved. It must have been the energy that protected it all these years. Isn't it weird, that even the elements of time can't penetrate it. Charlotte said, Isn't it unbelievable? Who would ever believe a story like this, if you told them? John looked at her and said, it really doesn't matter. I don't plan on telling anyone. Do you? Charlotte said, not on your life and they sat and watched as the energy circled the house.

Finally, John said, well I guess we better go home. Charlotte was scared, she felt great fear of the energy. She said, but how? John looked at her and said, we drive right through it. It hasn't hurt us yet, has it? She said, no I guess it hasn't. But John heard the terror in her voice. He reached over and drew her near to him and they slowly drove down the driveway. The closer they got to the house the more the energy became invisible. They got to the house and it was completely out of sight. They couldn't see it any longer but they both knew it was still there. They could hear the low hum that it made as it closed the house off from the outside world.

They got the car in front of the house. They were glad to be close. They ran hand in hand to the front door and hurried inside. John switched on the lights and they were both totally shocked. All the furniture was laying face down on the floor. The television was playing and laying on it's front. They walked through the hall to the kitchen and dishes were smashed all over the floor. The table was left standing upright but all the chairs were laying on their sides. On top of the table were the contents of the pantry. Flour and sugar was dumped in the middle of it and cereal was thrown all over the table and the floor. The whole kitchen was in a shambles. John said to Charlotte, well I guess we might as well start cleaning and went to the broom closet to get the broom.

Charlotte tried to save as many dishes as she could but there weren't many that were in one peace. They were both busy when John whispered, Charlotte and pointed to the table. There right in front of their eyes, they stood and watched someone writing on the table.

The letters appeared slowly and very scribble. They were printed in bold capital letters. "DON'T LEAVE ME." John looked at Charlotte and said, well at least we know what made her so angry. She must of thought we left her for good. Charlotte said, well no wonder she was so mad. She thought we ran out on her when she was so close to being at peace and at that point. Charlotte looked up in the air and yelled. Sarah, can you hear me? If you can, don't worry we're not leaving you. We said we would help and we intend to do just that. No matter what it takes. Just then a breeze blew through the kitchen and blew flour everywhere. When it settled, the words were gone and the two of them knew, they wouldn't have anymore trouble with Sarah. John by this time is finding all of this a little amusing. He said to Charlotte. Can you believe our luck? "We have a house. The house has a ghost and the ghost has an attitude". John no sooner got the words out of his mouth when all of a sudden a book came whizzing down the hall and through the kitchen door just missing his head. He said, Sarah I'm sorry. I was just joking, Honestly.

John looked at Charlotte and gave her a sheepish grin. Then came another cold breeze. Charlotte looked at John and said, now what. They heard something in the hall by the kitchen door but didn't see anything. Next they heard footsteps on the floor. There they both witnessed the tiny footsteps walk through the kitchen, over through the flour on the floor to where the book landed. The book floated up off the floor, back across the kitchen and back to the hall. John turned to Charlotte and said, I wonder if that means she excepted my apology? Charlotte said, as she smiled back. Yeah, I think so.

John and Charlotte still had a lot of work ahead of them so they made themselves busy. Both of them as they cleaned, thought Sarah is the one who made this mess and she should be the one to clean it. But neither of them had the nerve to say it, so they continued to get things back to normal. When the kitchen was almost done. Charlotte stopped and leaned against the mop. She said, you know what? I just thought of something. Why is it, that Sarah has never shown herself before tonight? Isn't it strange? John thought for a minute and said, no not really if you think about it. She said, what do you mean? He said, she's using you. Charlotte said, I don't understand what your saying. What do you mean she's using me? John said, she's using your strength. Remember what Mrs. Darcy said. She said that Sarah needed your physical form to weaken the wall of energy. So, maybe she's using you now and if she is she'll only become stronger. Charlotte thought for a minute and said, Yeah, Maybe your right. Now she and John had something to think about as they finished the kitchen.

They got the house back in order and by this time it was late. They were exhausted and went up to get ready for bed. After they laid down beside each other they laid in each others arms and went right to sleep. At three o'clock John was awaken by a noise. He didn't know where the noise came from so he rolled over towards Charlotte and discovered that she was gone. He looked around and saw her just as she started to go down the steps. He called to her, but she didn't answer him. He thought she didn't hear him, so he called to her again and still she continued down the steps.

John sat up on the edge of the bed and watched her. He thought that's strange, I know she must of heard me. So why didn't she answer me? He walked to the doorway and stood quietly. He noticed that Charlotte was acting strange. She was staring straight ahead and John thought she must be sleep walking. John was curious now and followed her. He was careful not to make any noise, he certainly didn't want to scare her, so he kept a safe distance. He followed her down the steps and out the front door. He called to her softly and this time she turned and looked at him. She motioned for him to follow her and he did.

Charlotte walked across the porch and down the steps and John thought how beautiful she looked in the moonlight. When Charlotte got to the walk she turned and again motioned for John to follow her and he did just as she wanted. She was headed towards the Rose Garden. John followed her, but still kept a safe distance. Charlotte got to the garden and when she got to the middle of it she dropped to her knees and by this time she was crying. She started to dig at the dirt with her bare hands. She dug furiously, crying all the while. John went to her to try and stop her, but it was no use. She fought with him and dug harder. John soon realized that there must be a good reason for her to be digging there. He ran to the house and got a lantern and shovel and went back to the garden. But when he got back, Charlotte had already found what she was digging for. John knelt down beside her to try and help her get control of herself. She was crying so hard, it became heart raking sobs. John's heart was breaking seeing his wife like this, but he didn't know what to do. He sat along side of Charlotte and wrapped his arms around her. After awhile he got the lantern and brought it close so he could see what she was digging for. When he shined the lantern towards to hole, he was horrified. There laying in front of him was the skull and what looked to be an arm bone of a human being. He couldn't believe his eyes. He ask himself, who can this be? He looked up at Charlotte and she began to weep quietly and all of a sudden she collapsed in his arms.

John picked Charlotte up and carried her out of the garden. He got to the benches by the well and sat down with her. He rested briefly and then carried her to the house. When he got there, he took her in and laid her on the sofa. He ran to the kitchen to get some water and when he returned, Charlotte was coming around. She was shocked to see where she was. She said, what am I doing here and how did I get here? What's happened? She looked down at her night gown and then her hands. She looked up at John with terror in her eyes and said, what the hell happened? John sat beside her to calm her and told her what they had found. He told her everything and they decided they had to call the police and that's exactly what John did. Fifteen minutes or so had passed and the police pulled into the driveway. They dug the rest of the remains up and took a statement from the couple. One of the officers who was very young and cocky found the story a little far fetched, but the next day made him a believer. The Lab. they sent the remains to, reported their findings. They said the skeleton was that of a young very petite female and that it was over a hundred years old. The cause of death was a fractured skull and a broken neck and with those type of injuries she was most likely murdered. Now they had to get in touch with Mrs. Darcy to see if the remains could be buried in the Tomb at the cemetery.

Because there was no doubt in John and Charlotte's mind that the skeleton was definitely that of Sarah's. It would be the proper thing to do, after all this time. Besides, half the Tomb was built for

Sarah anyway. After they contacted Mrs. Darcy and she okay-ed the burial. Her body wouldn't be released for a few days. So, a person is likely to think that from this time on things would get better. Well! They didn't. Sarah was at her worst.

Sarah got angrier, she moved all the furniture in the house. She stripped the blankets and sheets from the beds, she moved the clothes in the closets from one closet to another. She was constantly on the move. She built gigantic fires in the fireplace and threw wood all over the floor. For some reason unknown to John and Charlotte. Sarah was extremely aggravated. But Why? Her remains have been found and soon they'll be laid to rest in the Tomb with her loved one and still she's not satisfied. The days following only got worse. Charlotte has become almost a total stranger to John. She acts like she doesn't even know him, but there are times, "though far and few between" that Sarah disappears and Charlotte surfaces. But when this happens, it's only for a short time and when Sarah takes over again, John never sees her. She spends all her time up in the bedroom behind locked doors.

By this time, John is bewildered, he doesn't know quite how to handle the two personalities of his wife's so he stays away from the bedroom. He sleeps in the living room on the sofa. When he can sleep that is. The music is driving him crazy, there's no way to block it out. The music plays on and on and it plays what the old man called The Sweethearts Waltz. John still thought the music was eerie. The mandolins and fiddles played for hours and got very nerve racking. John thought it would drive him completely mad if it didn't stop soon and what made it worse was, he felt lost and alone without his Charlotte. Almost to the point that he couldn't deal with it any longer. Charlotte, on the other hand is doing quite well. She is her-self sometimes but Sarah is gaining strength. With each minute that passes she becomes stronger and strength is what she needs to weaken the wall of energy. The stronger she gets the weaker the wall gets and poor Charlotte is caught up in the middle of it all. But! Sarah needs Charlotte's strength to break down the wall and if she succeeds, then and only then, can she be with her loving Captain. Another night passes, John is getting extremely tired of all of this. He has a wife but never sees her and he feels so alone. She stays in the bedroom day and night. Charlotte doesn't even come out to eat or drink. He's worried about her, he walks up the steps to her door and stands quietly outside. He listens and hears her weeping. He has to keep telling himself, that it's Sarah and not Charlotte he hears otherwise he wouldn't be able to deal with it. He could never stand by and willingly watch while his wife was hurting. So, he told himself over and over, that it was Sarah crying.

John has had all of this torment he can stand for one day. He goes down stairs and gets his shower and goes to the sofa to bed. He laid quietly and watched T.V. and fell asleep while watching the news. Suddenly he was awakened by a loud bang. He was still half asleep when he came off the sofa. The noise was loud and startled him, he checked all around the house and noticed the front door was standing wide open. He ran to the door and out on the porch. When he got there he froze in his foot steps. He couldn't utter a word he was only able to stand and watch what was taking place. Charlotte was back up in the rose garden. The moon was shining bright and it was almost full. Charlotte was standing facing the cemetery. Her eyes never moved, she raised her arms and at this time, John witnessed something that he'll never forget. Charlotte was standing completely still, she looks like she might be in a trance of some kind and all of a sudden a form appears right in front of her. The form was facing Charlotte. When the form materialized completely John realized it was Sarah and for the very first time she appeared outside of Charlotte's body. Sarah stood and looked into the face that looked back at her. She reached out and took Charlotte by the hands and as she did Sarah merged into Charlotte's body. Like Mrs. Darcy said. Charlotte's body excepted Sarah willingly and from then on Sarah gained complete control and Charlotte was gone.

Chapter Eleven

THE CAPTAIN SPEAKS

John stands on the porch and as he witnessed that horrifying moment he dropped to his knees. He felt like his world has just come to an abrupt end. He stood by and watched as his wife completely transform into another woman. His heart is breaking and in his mind he thinking he's lost his wife forever. After he collects himself. He gets to his feet and walks towards the garden. He stumbled to the well and tried to keep his eyes on Sarah. He didn't want to miss anything that might take place from this time on. He got closer to Sarah and couldn't help thinking how very young and beautiful she was. He quietly moved closer to see what the young woman might do. He stood completely still and soon the music began to play. Sarah began to sway to the sound and soon she began to dance. She was doing the waltz and as she danced, she was beautiful and quite graceful. She looked as though she had danced the dance at least a thousand times.

John stood quietly and watched, he was waiting for Charlotte to return, but the music played almost all night. When finally the early morning came, the music stopped and Sarah stood still for the first time in hours. She walked towards John and went right past him. He turned and watched as she walked towards the well and around to the other rose garden. She turned and walked back to John and said, My dear man, what are you doing here? What is it that you want? And who are you? You know my Joe won't like this at all. You must leave if you value your life. Then she ran to the house and bolted the door. John ran after her to the house, he tried to open the front door but it was bolted. Sarah locked it from the inside and John didn't have his keys with him outside. He right away thought about the window. Thinking it may be unlocked, but when he got there and looked in. He completely forgot what he was there for. Sarah was in the study, she was pacing and as she went back and forth she was talking and at first John thought she was talking to herself, but then he saw the shadow of another person. He watched patiently hoping to get a look at the other person. He prayed all the while, hoping that it was the shadow of Charlotte. Soon John was very disappointed. The shadow of the other person was the little old man. John couldn't believe it. He said to himself, How in the hell did that little son of a bitch get in there?

John continued to watch, he saw them talking and put his ear against the glass to see if he could hear what they were saying. They went through all the motions of a conversation, but not a sound was uttered. They were communicating from the world of the Super Natural. Sometimes they spoke without even saying a word. John knew something was very wrong. Sarah began to pace faster, back and forth, back and forth and at that point, even a fool could see that Sarah was extremely upset about something. John strained to see if he could learn anything about what was going on in the house. Then all of a sudden his attention was directed somewhere else. He heard a loud high pitched buzz and then cracks, almost sounded like lightning as it strikes. John was startled by the noise. After he listened for a minute he thought maybe it was a short in a big transformer somewhere. Then he realized there was no transformers around. But, he did knew that the sound was ear piercing and it seemed to be coming from around the side of the house. He ran to the edge of the porch to look at the electric meter, he thought it may have shorted out and the noise was coming from there. When he got to the place where he could look out, he was totally shocked at the sight. His eyes followed the glow and slowly he looked out over the Cemetery. Everything out there was illuminated. There was a blue green haze that hung close to the ground and John couldn't believe his eyes.

Then suddenly the Wall of Energy appeared. It was truly a spectacular sight. John was breathless as he stood and watched the wall materialize. But soon he was brought back to the activities in the house. He heard the front door swing open. He stood quietly and waited, soon he saw Sarah approach the door. He noticed something strange about her. She wasn't walking, she was floating. She floated out on the porch and down the steps towards the Cemetery and John followed, but at a safe distance. He was careful not to get to close, he didn't want to interrupt what was about to take place. He was praying silently that maybe the end was near. Sarah floated out to the Wall of Energy. She stopped about five feet away from it and stared into the cemetery. She slowly raised her arms and turned her head to look towards the Tomb. John followed her eyes and looked just in time to see the Captain appear. He too, seemed to be floating. He moved slowly towards Sarah and as he was moving in her direction, he raised his arms in the exact same manner that Sarah had. It looked as though they were getting ready to embrace. They both began to move slowly towards the wall and when they were about five feet away from the wall, they stopped. The couple stood a looked at each other, their eyes met, but neither of them move. The Wall of Energy stood between them. John stood in the back ground. He watched and soon he was feeling great pity for the young lovers. He, for the first time, saw the torment on their faces and felt the pain they were feeling.

They were so close to each other, yet so very far away. They were so sad. All they wanted was to be together and at peace. Things came to a halt for the time being, Sarah and the Captain stood and looked at each other. The longing was almost to much for them to endure. Then suddenly they began to move. They slowly approached the Wall and when they got almost close enough to touch. All hell broke loose. Bolts of energy that looked like lightning shot out towards them. When it hit them they screamed with agonizing screams. The sound was ear piercing and John couldn't stand it. He dropped down on his knees in the grass. He tried to protect his face from the flashes and covered his ears with his hands. The flashes were burning his eyes, but he watched through squinted to see what was happening. He watched helplessly, then finally Sarah jerked herself free, then John took notice to the Captain. He looked as though he was determined to come through. He was almost to the middle of the wall when the noise and bolts of energy grew more intense. The sound was unbelievable, then the Captain was thrown through the air. The force was tremendous and he landed about middle ways of the Cemetery.

By this time, John was still on the ground, he couldn't believe his eyes. He never blinked, he had to see what Sarah was doing. He noticed that things began to quiet down a little and soon he was able to see Sarah clearly. She was on her knees by the Wall weeping as though her heart was breaking. She looked up into the Cemetery, just in time to see the Captain vanish into the heavy blueish green mist. John was stunned by everything that took place. He thought everything would be over and evidently the lost couple did too. But still the Wall of Energy is to strong. The spirits still can't penetrate it. But Why? They found Sarah's remains and still the Energy is to strong. John felt helpless as he sat there in the cold night air. He would give anything if he could only help Sarah right now. He would like to go to her and hug her and tell her everything would be okay. Her crying was breaking his heart. He has a very soft spot for a woman crying. He wanted to go to her but didn't dare. He knew she was a ghost and she didn't respond well to him. So he slowly turned to go back to the house before she locked him out again. When John got to the porch his heart was heavy, he was thinking about his wife and if he would ever see her again. He was trying to figure a way to help her come back. He walked through the entrance hall and looked into the study. There out cold on the floor, laid Charlotte. John ran to her saying, "Please God" let her be alive. When he got to her, he knelt down beside her, but hesitated to touch her.

Almost as though she was dead and he knew in his heart that, that was something he couldn't bare. He sat and stared at her, his mind racing. He was in a state of disbelief and he began to weep, as he wept, he bent over to embrace his loved one and laid his head upon her chest. Then and only then did he realized that Charlotte was still alive. He heard a faint heart beat as he pressed his ear to her chest and soon Charlotte began to breath. It took no time at all, until she was breathing normal. She moaned and opened her eyes. John was so happy he took her in his arms and cried like a baby. Charlotte reached up to touch John and said, Honey what's wrong, why are you crying? John pulled away in disbelief. He said, you mean you don't know?

Charlotte looked at John with a puzzled look on her face. John said, Honey do you remember anything about what just happened. Charlotte said, what are you talking about and then realized that she was lying on the floor in the middle of the study. She looked at her husband with a look that told John she had no idea what just took place. She didn't remember anything at all about her ordeal. John put his arms around Charlotte and helped her to her feet. She was extremely weak so he practically carried her to the sofa. Once he got there he sat her down and stayed close to her as he explained everything that happened. John finally finished telling the whole story and she sat and stared at the floor. She couldn't believe it, she was thinking. Now what? We thought we were so close to the end of all of this and something else goes wrong.

John and Charlotte talked for hours, they were trying to figure out what happened and most importantly, why. They finally came to the conclusion that there was more to it than they thought. But what? The only logical thing they could come up with was that it must have something to do with the Captain. After they finished their conversation they both walked outside to see if Sarah was still there. They opened the door to go out on the porch, Charlotte felt a deep sadness and took John by the hand. She stopped and John turned to look at her. She said, I don't have to see if she's there. She's gone, I can feel it. John took Charlotte in his arms and pulled her close, as he held her tight he said, come on I want you to see this. He held her hand and led her across the porch and down the steps to the walkway. All the time he was looking for Sarah and found that Charlotte was right. Sarah was gone. John still had Charlotte by the hand but he felt her tugging on it. She was lagging back and John turned to see why. She was looking out into the cemetery and to his surprise he saw the Captain standing, "once again," on the other side of the Wall of Energy. This time John noticed that things were a little

107

different. The Captain was weak, he was fading in and out but one thing was for sure. He was still suffering. In his eyes as he looked at John, he was pleading for help. John knew somehow what he was trying to say. He said to the Captain, How can we help? Tell us somehow, in some way what to do.

John was feeling great pity for the Captain, but had no idea at this point what else they could possibly do. He reached out to Charlotte who was lost in the moment. She was staring into the night, she too, was feeling hopeless. She looked up at John and he said, come on let's go to the house. We can't do any good out here and as they turned to go towards the house they both stopped instantly. Suddenly the music began to play and they both felt deep sympathy for the Captain as they slowly continued towards the house. John and Charlotte went to the kitchen once they got inside the house. They needed something to calm them down. They sat at the table and drank warm tea and noticed it was extremely quiet except for the music. It played on through the night and as John and Charlotte went to bed they fell asleep to the haunting sound of the Sweethearts Waltz. John was extremely tired and fell into a deep restful sleep, while Charlotte was quite restless, but soon John was woke up by the thrashing movements of Charlotte. She was tossing back and forth as she was kicking and hitting at something or someone. Suddenly she started to scream. She said, who are you and what do you want? At that point John tried to wake her, but she didn't wake up. She continued to talk in her sleep.

Her voice became very calm and she was speaking softly now. She was carring on a full conversation with someone. But John had no idea who she might be talking to and as he listened to one side of the conversation he soon realized that she must be talking to the Captain. In her side of the conversation, she was taking about some events that happened in the time of the Civil War. She was talking about Slavery and the Confederate States. John was confused by what she was saying, it was like she was living in the time. She talked on and on, most of which was rambling but finally she said, I love you Joe and fell into a peaceful sleep. John laid awake for some time watching Charlotte and thinking about the dream she must of had. It was very difficult for him to deal with the fact that his wife was dreaming of another man. Especially knowing the passion she felt for the Captain. He had to remember that his wife was being faithful to him and that Sarah was the one who was thinking about her lover. Finally he went to sleep, but was soon awaken by the warm sun shining in his face. He rolled over to say good morning to Charlotte and to his surprise she was gone. He immediately jumped out of bed and went on the hunt of her. He checked the bathroom and then went to the kitchen. There he found her sitting at the table drinking a cup of coffee. He walked over to her and put his arms around her from behind. He bent down to kiss her and was delighted she didn't pull away.

He knew right then, that it was Charlotte sitting there and not Sarah. He went to the sink and poured himself a cup of coffee. It was a tough night and he needed an eye opener. After he fixed his coffee to his taste he went to the table to sit down opposite Charlotte. He noticed she was extremely quiet. He tried to strike up a conversation but soon noticed that Charlotte was in another world. He sat and watched her for some time and all she did was sit and stare into her cup. Finally he said, Honey are you alright? She didn't answer, so he spoke more demanding. Charlotte! Did you hear me? "I said" are you alright? And only then did Charlotte hear him. She said, I'm sorry honey, I didn't hear you. I was thinking. John was feeling a little more at ease now at least he got her to talk to him. He said, what were you thinking about? She said, I was thinking about a dream I had last night. Their eyes met and John ask her if she wanted to talk about it. She said, yes I would like to tell you about it, it was so weird. It was almost like it was real. John reached across the table and took her hand. She started by saying the dream was almost like a dream she had a while back and she proceeded to tell him about the dream...

A man was laying face down in the mud. He was hurt somehow and was in agonizing pain. He thinks he's dying and as he lays there around him are three men. Their looking down at him and laughing at his misfortune. The man struggled to get his face from the muck but eventually he died. As he died his spirit lifted and next it came to me at the well. I was working in the roses when I first saw him. He was a horrible sight. His chest had a big gaping hole in it and he was covered with blood and dried mud. His face was bloody but even with all that he was smiling at me. He ask if he could draw some water from the well for he was very tired and parched. I helped him with the water and he sat down to rest. He sat quietly for a long time and finally he spoke. He spoke sofyly and pointed at the Tomb, he said the answers are there. They,ve been there for over a century. Then it was horrible, He turned to ashes right in front of my eyes and blew away. Charlotte fell silent, she was very confused by the dream. John on the other hand was very excited. He jumped up from the table and said, that's it, I knew it. The answers are in the Tomb. Maybe we'll be able to find the answers if we open the Tomb. He was excited and anxcious to get started. He wanted to go out and open it right away. Charlotte immediately jumped to her feet, she said, no! You can't. You have no right opening that Tomb without consent and the only one who can consent to that is Mrs. Darcy. John looked at her and said, OK, then we go to see her right now.

John went to the phone to call Mrs. Darcy. She answered and John told her what he had to and she told him that today was impossible, because she had an appointment for that afternoon. So they made arrangements to meet the next morning and hung up the phone. John went back to the kitchen to tell Charlotte that they could go and see her tomorrow. Charlotte said, but I don't think that's a very good idea. John said, what do you mean? I don't understand. Why not? Charlotte then reminded him about what happened the last time they both left the house. She said, maybe the next time it'll be worse. John looked at her with a stunned look on his face and said, man I totally forgot about that. He then said, OK, if we can't go to her, maybe we can convince her to come here. The morning came and John woke bright and early. He got breakfast and waited until nine o'clock to call Mrs. Darcy. He again explained everything that's been happening. She listened quietly as though she was very concerned. When John finished telling her everything, he ask if she would please consider coming to the house. She refused immediately. John pleaded with her to try and make her understand how desperate they were and finally she reluctantly said she would. John was relieved that she finally answered, he was about to give up and open the Tomb without her consent. But now she will be here to witness the opening. John went to pick up Mrs. Darcy and left Charlotte at the house. John got there and back as soon as he could and when they got back Charlotte was waiting for them. She invited in their guest and offered her some tea.

When she took care of her company she recommended they go to the living room to talk. John showed Mrs. Darcy to the living room and soon Charlotte came in with a tray of tea and cookies. When everyone got settled they began to talk. They talked about all the pleasant things first. The house, the rose gardens, the cemetery and then the conversation went to the Tomb. Now at this point of the discussion John took over. He told Mrs. Darcy that he believed that they could find the answers they needed in the Tomb. He also said, that until they find the truth the spirits won't rest. Mrs. Darcy was shocked at the suggestion. She said, Why on earth would you think such a thing? Besides the body of the Captain is at rest there and it wouldn't be right to disturb it after all these years. John was furious with Mrs. Darcy. He was pacing the floor as he said to her. How in the hell can you say something like that? The Captain is not at peace. Charlotte and I have both seen him and he's suffering like no poor soul should ever have to. All he wants to do is get to Sarah, but the Wall of Energy is still to strong. The whole truth is still not known and I truly believe the mystery lies out there in the Tomb. Mrs. Darcy was outraged, she said, "absolutely not" I won't permit it. It's not right. So at this point of the conversation Charlotte took over. She felt she had to because things were getting way out of hand. Both John and Mrs. Darcy were angry and they were getting no where fast.

Charlotte got Mrs. Darcy's attention by telling her that the Captain came to see her last night. Mrs. Darcy seemed surprised, but then she became extremely interested in what Charlotte was saying. She said to Charlotte, tell me about your dream. Charlotte stood up and started to pace as she began to speak. She started by saying, the dream was so real, it's hard to think of it as a dream. It started with the Captain and myself at the well and from that point on Charlotte told Mrs. Darcy the whole dream. After Charlotte finished she said, now can you understand why we need to open the Tomb? The answers must be there. The Captain pointed at the Tomb, he was telling us there was something hidden in there.

Mrs. Darcy sat quietly for a short spell and when she spoke again she said, Some time back, I too had a dream. And like your dream Charlotte, it seemed so real. The Captain was falling, he fell face down in the mud. He tried to free his face from the muck and when he finally got himself rolled over and his face free from the mud he looked up into the faces of three men. The men were making cruel jokes and laughing at the Captain's misfortune. The Captain laid there in the mud with blood all over him and in agonizing pain and as he died he was looking into the faces of three of his own men. The men were in his Regiment. Until now the dream didn't make any sense. Is it possible that those men had something to do with the Captains death? At this point of the conversation John had something to say. He spoke up and said, so you see that's all the more reason for us to open the Tomb. We'll have a Medical Examiner check the body to see how he died. Maybe that will give us a clue to what we're missing and finally after a little thought Mrs. Darcy agreed. The three talked until late evening. They had to decide the right way to go about opening the Tomb. There were legal procedures they had to follow and all they had to do was find out what they were. They talked about who they would contact.

Mrs. Darcy had some pretty important friends in high places, so they let her handle the talking. But for now, all they could do was wait until morning. It's very late and Mrs. Darcy said, I really should be going home. By this time John and Charlotte became quite fond of the little old lady. They enjoyed her company and invited her to stay the night. She refused of course, but they insisted. They said, if she stayed she would be here when everything began to come together. Mrs. Darcy gave it a little thought and then agreed to stay over. She thought the couple was right, maybe this way everything will be taken care of tomorrow. Charlotte showed Mrs. Darcy to the guest room and got her some things she might need for her stay over. When Charlotte got her guest settled in she said, good night to her and they all turned in for the night. "But not for long". Mrs. Darcy had just fallen asleep when she heard something. Charlotte and John heard the same thing and were brought to their feet. They knew right away what was happening. Sarah was on the move again and she seemed to be very disturbed about something. She was throwing things across the down stairs. The furniture was being upset and she was banging doors. Mrs. Darcy ran out into the hall to see what all the ruckus was about. By this time John and Charlotte were standing at the top of the stairs. Mrs. Darcy joined them and said, For the love of God, what's happening? John told her that it was Sarah and for some reason she's worse than ever. The three stood at the top of the steps and watched and listened. Every now and then they would see an object fly across the hall. Most of the time it was something breakable and it would shatter on the floor or the wall. Sarah is really angry this time and Mrs. Darcy spoke up and said, maybe it's me. Maybe she thinks I have no right being here, maybe I should leave. John said, No it's not you. She knows your here to help, so it has to be something else. Charlotte was extremely quiet, she stood by and watched her home being destroyed, but all she could think of was, Why, Why is she so angry. Then she realized and said, the anniversary date of the Captain's death is the day after tomorrow and Sarah knows the truth hasn't been found yet.

Charlotte began to walk down the steps. She took every step very slow, almost like she was unsure about going down. When she reached the bottom, she looked around to see if she could see anything. She evidently saw nothing and began to call out to Sarah. She said, Sarah can you hear me? I hope you can and if so, Please believe me when I say we're here to help you. I promise, we won't let you down. Just then the front door blew open and a cold bone chilling wind came rushing in. Charlotte ran to the door with John and Mrs. Darcy right behind her. They got out on the porch and the music began to play from the cemetery. As they looked towards the Tomb they saw the Wall of Energy appear once more. Mrs. Darcy was astonished at the sight, although John and Charlotte told her about the energy, she never imagined it would be so spectacular. She stood beside John and Charlotte as they all watched out into the Cemetery. Again Mrs. Darcy was amazed. For the first time she got the chance to see the Captain materialize from thin air, right in front of their eyes.

The Captain moved slowly as he came closer to the Wall of Energy. He stared at the three who were by this time down on the walkway. He never moved his eyes off of them. In his face they could see the pain and agony he was feeling. As he continued to stare at the three his facial expressions changed. He had the look of sorrow in his eyes and suddenly his mouth opened and for the first time the Captain spoke. He said, "HELP ME, PLEASE HELP ME" and as soon as he finished the words he vanished. It looked as though he used all his strength to utter those few words and he had to strain to do that.

Mrs. Darcy stood in disbelief, but she too was feeling great pity for the Captain. John looked over at her and he saw tears running down her cheeks. The Captain had gotten to her too. Finally she said, The poor soul is suffering so and he's my family. I could never rest knowing I could of helped and didn't. We have to put them to rest, no matter what it takes. But we have so little time she said, can we do it? John said, we'll give it everything we got. If the good Lords willing, we'll find the truth. As they all stared into the night each one of them was experiencing a feeling of total despair. But they knew they couldn't give up hope. They had to at least give it their best effort. John turn to go back to the house. He put his arms around both the women and led them away from the Wall of Energy. As they turned the ladies kept their eyes on the Cemetery. Possibly in hopes to see the Captain one more time. But for now, everything was at a stand still. Back in the house Charlotte looked around. The house was in total disarray. She was exhausted and told John that they could work on getting things cleaned up in the morning and they all went back to bed. Each one of them were feeling helpless at the time and they all had to take their heavy hearts and try to put them to rest for the night. The night was a long one. Out of the three of them, not one got an wink of sleep. Finally they one by one went down to the living room. They talked for almost the whole night, but when morning came they were sleeping on the sofa and chairs. When the sun finally came up it woke them. They each opened their eyes and were equally shocked. The house was completely put back in order. The furniture that had been broken was like it was before. There were no signs of damage. All the glass that was shattered in the hall was put back together and placed in it's original position. It seems that while they all dozed in the living room. Sarah paid them a quiet visit. The place was beautiful and spotless, she did in a short time what it would take one woman days to do. Mrs. Darcy was fascinated with the sight. She said, Sarah must believe that Joe is coming home and if she does, it means she trusts us. I think she knows now that we will do what ever it takes to free them.

John looked at the clock. Business hours have arrived and they were anxious to get started. They had a lot of calls to make and so little time to do it. But finally they got the numbers of the right people with the help of Mrs. Darcy's friends. Surprisingly, they had to make only one phone call and the Tomb would be open around noon. Everyone was happy about the arrangements, but very skeptical. If they couldn't find the truth. Then what?

How long would this continue to go on? Would there ever be peace for the two poor desperate souls? Each person in the house silently thought that they had to find the truth and they tried to think only positive thoughts. They all equally wanted desperately to find peace for Sarah and the Captain.

The morning passed quickly and before they knew it. It was noon. Charlotte was fixing lunch and when they all sat down to eat. Mrs. Darcy told them how much she was enjoying her stay and that it's the first time in years that she has really felt needed. She's been alone for so long that she is getting quite fond of having someone around who she can talk to and share her feelings with. She's grown very comfortable with John and Charlotte. So she decided to stay with the young couple until the whole sad ordeal was over with. John helped to clear the table and put the dishes in the sink. When he finished he went to get the dish rag to wipe the table and looked out the window. He saw a police car coming down the lane and a white van right behind it. He went to the door to let the men in. A police officer introduced himself and handed John some papers. As John reached up to take the letter from the officer. Their eyes met,

The officer told John that in the letter was the Court Order that they needed to open the Tomb. John read the contents of the letter and looked up at Mrs. Darcy.

He smiled at her and said, this is it, You did it. Your Judge friend signed it and we're ready to go. Mrs. Darcy was very pleased, she thought when this was all over she would have to call the Judge and thank him personally. He is a true friend, they've known each other since high school. She was a little older than the Judge and really didn't become friends until their early twenties. Their friendship developed into the kind that would last a life time and thanks to that friendship they now have what they needed to open the Tomb. The men ask John to show them the way. John grabbed his coat and said, this way. The women didn't want to miss anything so they got their coats on and followed them out to the Cemetery. The Medical Examiner drove his van carefully through the cemetery and around the outside edge until he got to the big willow tree. He saw the little old man standing in front of the Tomb. He turned to say to John, I didn't know you had someone waiting out here. I hope he hasn't been here long. John said, Oh no, he hasn't waited long. Only all of his life and smiled as he got out of the van. John didn't take time to explain his statement, he figured no one would believe him anyway. But the Examiner had his mind on something else anyway. He took his eyes off the little old man for just a few seconds and he was gone. He said to himself, I didn't see him walk away so where in the hell did he go and at this point he's thinking, the man just vanished.

John saw the look on the Examiner's face. He knew exactly what he was thinking and was just a little amused by it all. He thought, maybe he should explain but really didn't want to scare them off. There was very little time left and he didn't want to take the chance of losing their help. So, he decided not to say a word and hoped the little old man would behave himself until they got what they needed....

Chapter Twelve

THE TOMB

John was helping the Medical Examiner get his equipment from the van. Their pace was slow, neither one was in a hurry to get started at the gruesome task that lies ahead. Finally the assistants to the medical examiners showed up. They were late, so they pitched right in and helped finish unloading the equipment. Being late didn't seem to matter much. It was a chore that nobody was looking forward to. The police officer came in and went directly to the door of the Tomb. He helped by pulling all the brush away and clearing the door so it could be opened. By this time Charlotte and Mrs. Darcy walked around the Willow tree. When Mrs. Darcy got her first look at the Tomb she froze in her tracks.

She stood and stared at the door, she's never been this close before. She squeezed Charlotte's hand. Charlotte said, are you okay? She looked at Charlotte and said, I've never been better. You know, I have a real good feeling about this, I don't know why, I just do. Charlotte had a blanket and a folding chair in her arms. The day was cold and damp and she wanted to make sure Mrs. Darcy was warm and comfortable. She didn't need to be sick after all this and Charlotte got her sat down close enough that she could see what was happening. After they were comfortable they sat and watched in great anticipation. They were both very anxious to see the opening of the Tomb. The setting was perfect for this type of thing. The day was very damp, the sky was overcast and it was quite cold. It was like watching a movie. Everything was just a little eerie and the men who came to open the Tomb was feeling it too. They all seemed to be a little on edge. They had no idea why they were doing this, they only knew that they had a job to do. Finally the door to the Tomb had been cleared and to everyone's surprise the door was beautiful. The stone looked like they were just laid and the wood in the door looked like new cut wood.

The Examiner looked at the Police officer who was standing beside him. Then he looked at John and said, "very sarcastically". What the hell is this? Is this some kind of sick joke or something? This place was just built. It's not like you said it was at all. You said it was over a hundred years old. Your full of shit, this place was just put here. So," what in the hell" are you three up to?

John was speechless, He didn't know what to say at this point. He only knew that what ever he said, he had to be cautious. Then he realized he didn't have to say anything. He pointed to the lettering that was on the left side of the door. The Examiner followed John finger and saw something hidden in the moss. He cleared it away and found the inscription. It read.....

CPT. JOSEPH OWEN McMASTERS
B. Jan. 29, 1835
D. Oct. 20, 1861
Died at the age of 26 years young. Serving in the
Army of the Confederate States of America.

The Examiner read the name and dates. He turned to John and said, I can't believe this. He had a puzzled look on his face as he said, everything looks so new. How can this be? He looked at the officers and said, well! Shall we get started? Maybe we'll find some answers inside. They all hustled to get the Tomb opened. John stood back and watched. He found just a little amusement in the statement the Examiner made. It seems their all hoping for the same thing. "The answers that's hidden inside the Tomb and the stories that they might tell". After a lot of prying and pounding, they finally succeeded in opening the lock that was on the door. "Now the time of truth". The door swung open with ease and on the inside of the Tomb it was totally black. It was an eerie sight. The kind that made goose bumps go up your spine. One of the men lit the lanterns to make ready to enter the Tomb. When they were finished the Examiner said to John, I need you to come inside. We need you as a witness for when we open the coffin. John was paralyzed, he couldn't wait until this time had come and now that it has, he's extremely nervous.

He began to sweat and his hands were shaking. It's not fear he's feeling it's the thought of not finding what they need to free the Spirits. He looked over at Charlotte and she said, go ahead Honey we need to do this. You know we do. John realized at this point he had to clear his mind and get this thing over with. Charlotte was right of course, if they ever wanted to live peacefully in the house they had to do this. John swallowed hard as he walked towards the entrance. He slowly bent over to enter through the door and turned to look at Charlotte. She nodded at him to reassure him that it was alright and he turned to disappear inside the Tomb. As John entered the Tomb, he had a hard time seeing. It took a few seconds for his eyes to adjust to the darkness. But when they did, he was totally astonished at the sight. The Tomb was Hugh, it measured approximately 20 ft. by 20 ft. John thought it didn't look near this big from the outside. Each of the walls had windows built in to them.

The windows were all stained glass and each one had angels in the center of them. The windows were beautiful, John never seen anything like them in his life. He was thinking what a waste. The windows couldn't be seen at all from the outside. Their beauty was completely hidden from the world outside. John got his mind off the windows and back to the reason he was there in the first place, but it was difficult. "The Tomb being what it was". On the left side of the Tomb stood the statue of a soldier and behind the statue was a coffin. From there Johns eyes slowly scanned the rest of the Tomb. He looked at the coffin from the bottom to the top and continued on around the walls to the center in the back. There stood the statue of an angel. Her arms were extended and in her hand she held a little golden box. John moved close enough to see the box and discovered it was a music box.

At this point John became very curious, he was wondering if the box was the reason for the music they've been hearing. He had to know, so he walked towards the statue. His hand was trembling as he reached out to touch the little box and sure enough as soon as he touched it the music started to play. The music was exactly what John thought it would be. The Sweethearts Waltz. Every person in the world has experienced at one time or another what John is feeling at this moment. Chills have run through his body and he's not sure what to do. Turn and run or stay and pay the price. At this point John decides he has to stay and find out everything about the Captain. He turned to examine the rest of the Tomb and to his amazement he see's another coffin. But who's? He knows Sarah was never laid to rest, they found her remains in the garden. So who does the coffin belong to? John turned to one of the men who was holding a lantern and ask if he could come close enough so he could read the inscription. The man came close and they found the casket to be one of the most beautiful coffins to ever be made. It had a half lid and was made of bronze. On the top half of the lid was a gold plaque that read...

The final resting place of;
SARAH JANE BRAIDEN
B. Mar. 28, 1837
D. Nov. ____, 1861
MAY GOD GRANT HER PEACE AND LOOK OVER
HER. UNTIL SHE'S LAID TO HER FINAL REST.

John felt saddened, he now knows he's standing there looking down on an empty coffin. After he read the inscription he realized they may be able to lay Sarah to rest. They found her remains and were going to bury them in the cemetery, but this is where she's supposed to be and this is where she'll go. While John was intrigued with Sarah's empty coffin, the Examiner was ready to open the Captain's coffin. He walked over just as they were opening the lid. He felt a cold breeze and got chills up and down his spine. He had no idea what to expect, he's never done anything like this before and before now he never cared to. He was expecting the worst. In his mind he pictured a body that was decomposed and imagined it to be something like out of a horror movie. But, as the lid opened he saw exactly what everyone else did. There in the coffin laid the body of a man who was completely preserved. It looked as though he had just been placed there. John just stood and stared into the coffin. He was puzzled, he was thinking, why was the Captain completely preserved when Sarah's body was decomposed. All they found of Sarah was her skeleton. Then he thought about the house and the Tomb, they too were completely preserved. But Why? What's the reason for it. And then it dawned on him that Sarah was buried outside the bubble of energy. Now he knows that the Wall of Energy is the reason everything is completely preserved.

While John was preoccupied with his thoughts the Examiner was checking the casket and the body. He too, was equally puzzled about the condition of the corpse, but he said that it being in the condition it's in makes things much easier. He decided to do his job right there in the Tomb. He also figured he knew what to look for so he would be finished in no time at all. The Examiner reached into the coffin with his hands covered with rubber gloves. He pulled the blanket that was covering the Captain all the way to the bottom of the casket. Exposing the body completely. The captain was laid to his final rest in the same uniform he died in. It still carried all the medals and stripes he was awarded. He must have been an outstanding soldier. Who ever laid this man to rest, must have done the best they could do with the uniform. It still had some signs of mud and stains and there was no mistaking, the stains on the front in the chest area were blood stains. The whole chest and down the front of the trousers were stained with blood. The jacket in the front was filled with small holes. The Examiner unbuttoned the jacket to expose the chest and found an undershirt. As he cut the shirt away, he found gobs of dried blood and flesh. He continued to remove the shirt and soon exposed the whole upper portion of the body and right in the center of the chest was a hole the size of a dinner plate. John at this point was feeling a little nauseated, He was thinking, it must have been a miracle that the Captain lived long enough to write to Sarah before he died.

The pain he must have felt as his life was slipping away. But soon John was brought back to reality and his thoughts just drifted away. The Examiner was ready to roll the body over to see what the back of the corpse looked like. He took his knife and cut the jacket clear up the middle. He needed to remove the jacket completely and this was the easiest way. As they pulled the jacket off the Captain, they did it carefully. There was no disrespect at all to the dead as they removed one half of the jacket at a time. When they rolled the body to remove the last half of the jacket and lifted it away. John noticed something had fallen on the body. He looked closer and saw that they were some type of papers.

As the men were busy examining the body. John slipped on some gloves and carefully reached in to grab the papers. As soon as he got the papers in his hand he turned to go outside to the light. The Examiner ask where he was going and made a comment about him being weak and the other men laughed as John ran out the door. When he could see the papers he saw that there was a letter in them. The letter was addressed to Sarah. It read......

> Nov. 19, 1861
> My dearest Sarah,
>
> Counting the hours until we're together again. All I can think about these days is your smiling face. The love I feel for you is the only thing that keeps me going in this ugly war. It seems I not only battle on the fields but in our Winter Quarters too. You see, There are some men in my Regiment who for some unknown reason hate me. The lord only knows why. I've tried everything humanly possible to win these men over but their hate runs to deep. I was walking through camp on yesterdays eve when I came upon three men in conversation. I usually wouldn't of paid any mind, but the name Auggie Denton came up. They said Auggie would pay good money to the man

who put a bullet in my head. Then I realized why I was having such a hard time with these men. As it works out, Russ Jacobs is the brother of Auggie's best friend and I suspect he will make an attempt on my life. But don't you worry your pretty little head. I'll take particular care not to put myself at their mercy and besides in a couple of days I'll be home with you in the safety of your arms. My Love, I have to close for now. My orders just came in and we move at first light. Good night My Love.

Your Truest Love
Joe

P. S.
Look pretty, in three days I'll be home to you soon.

Charlotte stood and watched John as he read the paper. She was curious to find out about it, but she was reluctant to get any closer to the Tomb. She felt safe at a distance, but when she saw the look on John's face after he finished reading. He was stunned and she knew then he found something important. John dropped his arms down in front of him with the paper still between his hands. He looked up at Charlotte as she walked towards him. He was speechless. Charlotte said, what is it? John reached the letter out to her and she looked at it. She was equally shocked to see it was a letter of the Captain's. As she was reading the letter, John said, the Captain was right all along. The answers we were looking for were hidden in the Tomb all these years. The letter tells who killed him, if he was murdered and we'll know for sure real soon, how he died. John left Charlotte standing there holding the letter. She looked up at him, but couldn't say a word. John turned and walked back to the entrance and disappeared out of sight. He got back just in time to hear the men discussing the cause of death. The Examiner saw John as he walked back inside. He said, come on over and I'll show you what we found. He showed John two bullet holes in the Captain's back. The first one he pointed to was in the mid section of the back. He said, this was a bad hit for a man to take but it's not the one that killed him. This one is, and pointed to the upper left shoulder. There just below the shoulder blade was a small hole. The Examiner said, this is the fatal hit.

The bullet entered here and in the process it tore out half the lung and blew out the entire heart. So there is no doubt at all, that this man was shot in the back and probably died instantly. John was standing just staring at the body. The Examiner said, my guess is that this man was murdered, because a man in battle should be shot in the front. Unless he was a coward of course and was running from the enemy. Which in this case is very unlikely, seeing that he's a captain and in my opinion cowards don't make good Captain's.... Now that they found what they were looking for, the casket was closed and sealed once again. This time forever. All the secrets that were hidden there are now known and "hopefully", by the right people. And now maybe, since the truth is known. The Spirits will be able to go to their final rest.

Chapter Thirteen

A HORRIBLE DEATH

The tomb was closed but not sealed. Sarah's body will be placed there as soon as their finished with the examination. Which will hopefully be in a couple of days and then maybe it will all be over. All the men gathered their tools and put them into the van. By this time the sun has gone down and it's getting quite cold. It's around 5:30 in the early evening and the daylight will soon be gone. John and Charlotte had to get Mrs. Darcy back to the house before dark. She was almost froze, but refused to leave until she found out what was going on. She was anxcious to find out the results. She too, has waited a long time for the mystery to be solve and prays that now it might be finally over. They got Mrs. Darcy back to the house after quite a struggle. She was so cold she could hardly walk. So, at the end of the Cemetery, John picked her up and carried her to the house. When they got there he built a fire in the fireplace. Mrs. Darcy sat close to the fire while Charlotte went to the kitchen to start supper. After she started everything cooking she made tea and took it to the livingroom. She too, was chilled to the bone. The room was beginning to feel cozy and warm. The women sat by the fire and got comfortable while John went outside to get some fire wood.

When he finished he joined them. He could relax now, he had a beautiful fire in the fireplace and in no time at all the house began to get warm and cozy. John puttered around the fireplace for awhile and when he finished he got his tea and joined the women. He sat quietly and listened as they chattered back and forth. Then he joined in their conversation. He said Ladies, I don't know about you, but I'm feeling pretty darn good right now. Charlotte said, oh you are, are you and why might that be? She was joking with John again. He said yeah, don't you?

We've accomplished something today, we found the answer to something that's been unsolved for over a century and personally I feel real good about it. Now the Spirits can rest and as soon as Sarah is placed in the Tomb. It'll all be over, "Thank God". Charlotte sat and just listened to John as he spoke. Finally she said, John all of what you say is true, but you forgot one small detail. He said, what's that? She said, we still don't know who killed Sarah or how she died. John got a strange look on his face and in a slightly higher tone said to Charlotte. What about the man in your dreams and the flashes. Don't forget about the flashes. You said yourself, he was the man who killed Sarah. At this point Charlotte snapped back. She said, yes I told you what I saw. But, who was the man and why did he murder her?

He wanted her for his own, he said he loved her and wanted her for his wife. So, why would he want to kill her? John got real angry. He was almost screaming when he said to Charlotte. You know, if I didn't know any better, I'd think you were enjoying all of this. Well personally, I'm not. I'm tired of not sleeping, I'm tired of not going to work and most of all, I'm tired of not having my family together. I want to live like normal people and I'm fed up. If this thing isn't over in a couple of days. I'm leaving and I'm taking the kids. I'll go stay with my folks. "At least there I'll be able to sleep."

Charlotte looked at John with tears in her eyes. She said, Honey your tired and I'm sorry if I upset you. I just wanted you to realize that it might not be over. Only time will tell. Please hang in there, just a little while longer. Please! For me? And through all of this Mrs. Darcy didn't say a word. She sat by the fire in the rocking chair and stared at the hot amber's. Suddenly she stopped rocking and said, You know John, I don't want to intrude, but Charlotte may be right. I've been sitting here trying to figure this out. The Captain died on the twentieth, which is tomorrow and Sarah died two or three days later. So, if that's true, then anything could happen in the next few days. John listened to Mrs. Darcy and then realized how childish he was. He thought, I've been here through it all, so what's a couple more days. He looked at Charlotte and said, okay I'll stay and instantly Charlotte began to feel better.

She was beginning to think that John was going to run out on her, but she knows now he'll be here until it's all over and when it is, they can live in peace in their beautiful home.

Charlotte was feeling pretty content with their conversation. She went to the kitchen and soon they were at the table having their evening meal. Their conversation was mostly about their life on the West Coast and the children. They all tried very hard to avoid the subject of the spirits that were roaming the grounds and after a hearty meal, John escorted Mrs. Darcy back to the living room. Charlotte told them to go in and relax and she would clean the kitchen and join them. Charlotte was cleaning the table off and was thinking how tired she was. She couldn't wait to go and relax by the fire. She was almost finished when she started to feel a headache coming on. She took some aspirin for the pain, but it didn't help, it only became stronger. So she staggered to the table to sit down. She thought if she sat down and relaxed the pain would lessen, but she was wrong. The pain became excruciating and she screamed for John. John heard Charlotte's scream and ran to the kitchen. When he got there he saw her laying on the floor. He ran to her and called for Mrs. Darcy. She immediately got up from the rocking chair and ran as fast as she could to the kitchen. She stood over Charlotte and watched as John knelt down to try and pick her up from the floor.

And suddenly right in front of their eyes, Charlotte once again transformed into Sarah. John tried to hold her, but she pulled away. She was rolling all around on the floor screaming and kicking. She was muttering something that sounded like, Why are you doing this? You don't treat someone you love like this. Then suddenly her head jerked. It was like something hit her hard in the face. She then rolled up in a ball and cried like a baby. John stood in disbelief, he moved in a jester like he was going to help her, but Mrs. Darcy stopped him.

She said, she has to fight this battle alone. You can't help her. And battle it was. Sarah was struggling with someone or something. But why? The struggle went on for about ten minutes. John was in tears, he couldn't stand not being able to help his wife. Her clothes were torn and she was bleeding. The blood was soaking into her clothes and all over the floor. Finally she stopped struggling, she looked exhausted. She laid on the floor crying and was pleading for who ever was punishing her to stop. Finally she struggled to her feet and said, Auggie for God's sake, why are you doing this? Then her head jerked so hard it looked as though it would come right off her shoulders. She fell back to the floor. Her body was all twisted and she looked as though she was dead. John by this time is totally beside himself.

He runs towards her to try and help but was shocked when he saw her body being lifted off the floor. Some invisible force had her and was carrying her out through the kitchen. John at this point was horrified, he wanted in the worst way to help but was afraid of endangering the life of his loved one. He couldn't see Charlotte right now but he knew she was there inside of Sarah. So he just stood by and watched the lifeless body go right past him and out through the entrance hall. Once Sarah's floating body got to the door it swung open with a bang. Slowly Sarah disappeared into the night. John ran to the door and started to go outside when Mrs. Darcy's voice stopped him. She said John you can't interfere, if you do she might die. John was terrified as he ran out the door with Mrs. Darcy right behind him. They got to the edge of the porch and watched as Sarah's body floated towards the rose garden. They followed from a safe distance. When the force got Sarah's body to it's destination it dropped her to the ground. She hit hard, when she hit the ground her body made a terrible thud. Then John stood in total shock. The ground right beside Sarah's body began to open. There was no signs of anyone or anything being there, but still the ground was being dug. Soon there was a hole big enough to fit the body that lays waiting to be buried. John was felling helpless as he stood and witnessed the madness. He's being torn apart. If he helps his wife he takes a chance of destroying her and if he doesn't he'll lose her anyway.

He wept as he stood by and did nothing and then he began to pray. He said, Dear God, help her, I don't want to lose her, Please help her. And as he prayed he watched as her body once again left the place where it was thrown. It was lifted and this time was thrown in the shallow grave that had been dug. Her body hit the ground so hard she moaned. Her head and legs were twisted and one arm was behind her. She tried to speak and when she opened her mouth the dirt was thrown in on her. It hit her in the face and she screamed. She's alive, but still the dirt keeps coming. Her face and head was almost completely covered. She was fighting to get out but something was holding her down. She got her head free enough to scream. Auggie why are you doing this? I won't tell anyone what happened. I promise they won't know. I won't tell. Please Auggie don't do this, Please, please, please.

Then Sarah went silent for the last time, She was dead and Auggie killed her. When the grave was completely covered the earth stopped moving. John was terrified, he was praying it wasn't to late. He ran to the grave and dug at the top to free Sarah's head from the dirt. He saw her flesh and cleared the earth from around her mouth. She didn't move and John dug furiously. He was crying and saying, No you can't let her die. Help me God, Help her. You can't let her die. Then suddenly Sarah gasped for air and it was the most beautiful sound John had ever heard. She was alive...

John dug until he freed her hands then he grabbed her and pulled her from the dirt that covered her body. As John pulled her out he lifted her to carry her to the well and right there in his arms she transformed back to Charlotte. When he got to the well he sat her down on the bench, but she wouldn't let him go. She put her arms around his neck and held on for dear life. She said, Hold me please, I'm so scared. I thought I died in that hole. John brushed the dirt away from her eyes and mouth and kissed her. He said, everything's going to be okay, we know now that Sarah died in that hole. Auggie Denton killed her and worst of all, he buried her alive... Charlotte held on to John like she'd never let go. As he sat to comfort her with his embrace, she cried like a baby. Finally Charlotte was calm enough to speak. She said, My God, what a horrible way to die. No wonder she's so angry. He stole the very breath she breathed and there's no way to avenge her death after all this time. Mrs. Darcy didn't want to interfere, but now that it's over she went to Charlotte and said, come along dear, let's go get you cleaned up. She took Charlotte by one arm and John got the other as they held her on her feet and led her towards the house, but she was so weak that about halfway John had to carry her. As soon as they got to the house Mrs. Darcy drew a hot bath. John helped undress her and got her to the tub.

As she slid into the hot water soothed her aching flesh. Charlotte laid in the hot tub and let the dirt just soak away. She was exhausted and tried to relax. Soon she dozed off and fell into a deep, deep, sleep. Meanwhile Mrs. Darcy is in the bedroom waiting for her. About a half an hour passed and she called to Charlotte. But she got no response, so she called to John to come quickly. She told him that Charlotte doesn't answer her. He ran up the steps and into the bathroom. As he swung the door open he saw her sitting in the tub sound asleep. She was turning blue from the water being so cold, so he got her from the tub and dried her. He wrapped her in a bath blanket and carried her to bed. He covered her with a heavy comforter and sat down beside her just to look at her. He bent down and kissed her forehead and said, I love you. He watched her for a little while as she slept and thanked God she was alive. He then went down to join Mrs. Darcy in the living room. When he finally got comfortable. The two talked for hours in front of the fire. They talked until the wee hours of the morning. Mrs. Darcy was in her glory telling John all about her life and John enjoyed all of her stories. The fire was getting low, so John put some more wood on it. It was blazing in no time at all and at that point they just sat and watched the shadows of the fire dancing on the walls. The room once again became warm and cozy. It was the perfect setting for the music to start to play, and that it did. It was as though the atmosphere summoned it and when it played it played long and loud.

John looked at Mrs. Darcy. He then dropped his head down and covered his ears with his hands. He tried to drowned out the music because he knew it meant trouble, Sarah would be returning. Like she did all the other times when the music played. But when? He raised his head and tilted it to one side. He was listening for something. He heard something upstairs and looked over at the staircase. He walked over to the steps and started to go up, but he moved very slow. He took one step at a time, as though he was afraid of what was up there. When he reached the top step he stopped and turned to look down at Mrs. Darcy at the bottom. He then turned around and slowly walked over to the bedroom door. He stood outside quietly and listened and from behind the door he heard laughter, a woman's laugh. He listened for a short time, he wanted to go in, but couldn't bring himself to open the door. He knew he couldn't interfere and decided to ignore what was happening. So, He turned and walked back down the steps. In the bedroom Charlotte was asleep. She was laughing in her dreams. But soon she awoke from the pain she was getting in her head. She got out of bed and went to the dressing table to get some medicine for her headache. But the pain was so severe that she collapsed before she got there. She was unconscious for a short time.

When she woke up she pulled herself to her feet. As she did she leaned against the dressing table. When she got her head clear enough to think she looked into the mirror. As she looked at her image she took on another personality. Sarah has once again returned. She said with a giggle as she looked at herself. Sarah, My Dear, What on earth have you done to your hair. She sat down at the dressing table and began to fix her hair. When she was finished, it looked exactly as it did when she was alive. Next she went to the closet to get something to wear. She open the door and was shocked at what she found. Only Charlotte's clothes were there. She was extremely discouraged with everything she saw hanging in front of her until finally she found Charlotte's wedding gown. She took it out and looked at it, she held it to her and looked in the mirror. She said to herself, this is not exactly what I expected, but will have to do for the occasion. She slid off her nightgown off her shoulders and it slid to the floor and put the gown over her head. It fit perfectly, like it was made for her. Now she was dressed and ready. She went to the Balcony doors and reached out to open them. As they opened she felt the cold wind hit her face. It took her breath away, but she continued to open the doors. When they were completely opened, she then turned and went back to sit on the edge of the bed. She was now waiting for her lover.

The music began to play louder, it was almost ear piercing. Sarah stands up slowly and extends her arms towards the doors. Soon the Captain materialized right outside. He entered the room and went straight to Sarah. He embraced her and they both softly sat down on the bed. They sat side by side and carried on a complete conversation, like they must have done when they were alive. It was as though they picked up their lives right where they left off. Shortly, the Captain stood and turned to Sarah. He pulled her to her feet and kissed her and told her he would love her until the end of time and slowly walked away. He was going back towards the doors when the sky lit up. The Captain at this point turned back to look at Sarah and as he did flashes of energy came right through the doors and wrapped itself around the Captain. When it had him securely in it's grip, it swooshed right back out the doors, over the Balcony and back to the cemetery. Sarah ran to the balcony. She saw what was happening and screamed and as she did she collapsed on the balcony floor. John heard the scream from upstairs, he ran up the steps and opened the bedroom door. It was freezing in the room and he soon knew why. The balcony doors were wide open and Charlotte was lying on the outside. He ran to her and was stunned to see her in her wedding gown. He raised her in his arms and returned her to bed and quickly returned to close the doors. As he turned to go back to Charlotte.

He stopped to just looked at her. She was beautiful lying there in her gown of white, but she was also freezing. He went to the bed to cover her and sat down beside her. She was stirring and he knew she was okay. Soon she opened her eyes and looked up at John. She said hi, as she burst with excitement. She sat up on the bed and said, "he was here, he was here". John said, who was here? She said, the Captain he was in this room. John said, are you sure? How do you know? She said, I remember him being here. He came to tell Sarah how much he loved her, he kissed her and turned to go. He got almost to the doors, when suddenly the Energy oozed in, wrapped itself around him and literally drug him away. Just then Charlotte crumbled, she slouched over and cried uncontrollable sobs. She got to her feet and ran to the doors screaming, "Why? Why? Why did it take him? What's wrong now"? All the truth is known and still they can't be together. Tears were flowing freely down her cheeks as she turned to look at John, she looked deep into his eyes and dropped her head, and he knew she felt as though they failed the young lovers. She took a step to go back to the bed and her foot got tangled in her gown. She stumbled and quickly got control to avoid falling, then she realized she was wearing her wedding gown. "She was stunned", she looked at John hoping for some answers, but he too, was equally puzzled. She said, What in the "hell" am I doing with this on? John said, I don't know I thought I'd ask you, but I guess that won't do any good...

Will it? John slowly walked over to the doors, when he reached them, he turned to look at Charlotte. Their eyes met and he knew he had to go and see what was outside. He turned back around and went out on the balcony, as he walked to the rail he saw a very familiar sight. The Energy once again hovered over the house and cemetery. He was standing in the heavy green mist and suddenly got an eerie feeling. He looked out towards the cemetery and in the middle of it stood the apparition of the Captain and he was watching the balcony. John looked back at Charlotte and thought, was he really here, or was she just dreaming?

John stood in the cold mist and watched the Captain, He felt as though he was expecting something to happen, but had no idea what. He made a waving motion to the Captain and to his surprise, the Captain waved back. John couldn't believe his eyes, the Captain never tried to make any kind of contact until now. John waved again and the apparition just stood there and stared at him. John hopelessly stood there and tried to solve the mystery of it all, but after awhile he turned and went back into the bedroom with Charlotte. Charlotte was in the closet when John went back into the room. She got the gown hung back up and had her robe on. She was feeling pretty much herself by now and John was satisfied with that. Charlotte said, I'd like to have some tea and asked John if he would care for a cup. He said, I'd rather have a good cup of coffee and smiled at her.

She smiled and grabbed his hand and down they went to join Mrs. Darcy. They went to the kitchen and to their surprise Mrs. Darcy had coffee made and the tea kettle was boiling. "She is an amazing woman". She also had the fire in the living room roaring. She could certainly take care of herself for her age. When Charlotte sat down at the table she sat a cup of tea in front of her and said, here you are Dear, this will help calm you. I've added a secret ingredient to it, sip it slowly and soon you'll begin to relax. Charlotte sipped the tea slowly, her hands were trembling from her ordeal, but soon she began to feel better. When she finished, John said to Mrs. Darcy. Would you like to see the Captain? She answered with excitement in her voice. Yes, is he here? John said, sure is. He's right outside, at least, I think he's still here. Mrs. Darcy ran to the closet and grabbed her coat. They all walked out on to the porch. They went over to the rail at the side of the steps and John pointed to his right. Mrs. Darcy's eyes followed his and she gasped. The sight before her took her breath away. She said, Good Lord! as she stood and took in every small detail. What a spectacular sight. I've never in all my years, seen anything quite like it and she just stood and watched in complete silence. After a long period of time had passed.

Mrs. Darcy said, you know it's really sad when you stop and think about it. Out there stands a young man, or at least he looks like a young man, but he's not really. Now it's the soul of a young man who once existed in our world, and with extreme sadness in her voice she continued to say. Now I'm not sure what he is. He's trapped between the here and the here after, and he's in the worst kind of agony any being, living or dead can endure. He's so close to his eternal peace yet he's still unable to rest... Why? What's the answer's we're looking for? We're missing something... But what? Just then the Energy disappeared, but not for long. It became visible once again, but heavier this time. The Cemetery became illuminated once again and the heavy mist hung over the Tomb like a blanket. The Captain becomes stronger in appearance as he moves slowly towards the wall of energy. When he got as close as he dared to, he stopped and motioned for them to look at the Tomb... But why? What was he trying to say? John walked down the steps and slowly went towards the energy. He was careful not to get to close. He wasn't quite sure what kind of impact the energy would have on the living flesh. The sound alone was enough to make anyone with any sense at all, run the other way. It sounded like electricity, thousands of volts that once together formed a barrier to rise up and divided into two separate parts. One part formed a bubble around the house and the other went in the direction of the cemetery. It seemed as though the energy was there to protect and preserve everything that was inside, and the most amazing part is that it never hurt John or his family.

It's almost like it knows their there to put an end to all the suffering. John watched the energy, his eyes capturing the smallest of details as he followed it all the way around the house then he realized something. He said, "Well, I'll be damned"... Charlotte and Mrs. Darcy were standing right behind him and Charlotte said, what? what's the matter now? He looked at her and said, I just realized something that I don't think any of us gave any thought to. "Charlotte was anxious to find out what it was that John was thinking". She said, what are you talking about? He said, come look and I'll explain. John said, I was standing here looking at the haze the energy leaves behind, then it dawned on me. Did either of you stop to think about the fact that when we found Sarah's body. It was completely decomposed. While the Captain, who was less than the length of a football field away, was completely preserved. The women were spellbound, Charlotte said, your right... But why? John then walked between the women and took them by their arm and swung them around. He said look, then pointed to the rose garden. Their they all stood and stared, they were speechless. Finally Mrs. Darcy said, that's simply amazing. The rose garden is just outside the wall of energy, and it seems that Sarah's body being buried in the garden has gone through all the normal stages of death.

Where on the other hand, the Captain was protected by the shield of energy that hovered over the Cemetery... But why? There's got to be a reason for the energy to stop right there. She stood quietly for some time thinking about all the prospects. Then she said, It's like there's some sort of evil there and the energy wouldn't go close it. Charlotte looked at John and said, maybe she's right. Maybe there is some evil force out there and it had to be destroyed. John's had enough for tonight, so he put his arm around her and they headed towards the house. As they were walking he glanced towards the rose garden and said, That's probably something we'll never know... When they got to the steps of the porch, Charlotte stopped to look back at the cemetery. To her surprise, the wall of energy had disappeared. She said, look the energy's gone. John looked and said, "well I'll be". I wonder what it means? Maybe it's starting to weaken and they turned back around and went to the house. They all needed to get some rest. Once they got to the house they turned in and the rest of the night was extremely quiet...

Chapter Fourteen

THE HIDDEN TRUTH

The next morning brought beauty to the land. It was a glorious day and the twentieth of November. The anniversary date of the Captain's death. Things seemed to be peaceful as the day progressed. "But not for long". Around noon Charlotte went in to clean the living room while John and Mrs. Darcy recapped the night before in the kitchen. The were trying to sum up all the clues they had so they might know what to expect. Suddenly, the music began to play. It started off softly and the longer it played the louder it got, and John knew in his heart that Sarah has returned...

He ran through the hall to the living room door just in time to watch the transformation once again. She was fussing with her hair as she hummed the tune. She looked down at her clothes and was very unhappy about what she was wearing. Charlotte had on her long robe and when Sarah arrived it didn't suit her taste. But it really didn't seem to matter much because soon Sarah was completely enchanted by the music. She began to sway to the sound and soon she was waltzing around the room. She danced and danced and suddenly the room became extremely cold. A mist formed in the center of the room and in it's midst the Captain began to appear.

He was extremely weak, the upper half of his body appeared first. It faded and in a short while the lower half appeared right in front of Sarah. It slowly faded too, but Sarah continued to dance like the Captain was there with her and he probably was because she danced and danced. The look on her slightly transparent face was the look of total content.

John has forgotten for the time being that his wife is actually the one doing the dancing. He was enjoying the happiness that Sarah was feeling. Suddenly the front door blew open with a terrible crack. It startled John and he turned to see what happened. As he looked he saw coming through the door a greenish blue mist. It came through the entrance hall and right past John to the living room. Once it got there it wrapped itself around the invisible form of the Captain and a human form took shape. The form was moaning as the energy pulled it away from Sarah. The Captain was trying to hold on desperately, but the energy was to powerful and like a flash it once again pulled him away and carried him out through the door to the outside. John watched Sarah as she crumbled to her knees. She wept as though her heart was breaking. He looked back to the door and the whole world outside was lit up in a blue green haze. It looked like the end of the world has come, but John knew it was the Wall of Energy that has returned once more.

John stood staring, he was in total shock. Charlotte told him that the energy came once before but he never imagined it would be like this. At this point he began to lose grip. Mrs. Darcy saved him by her soft tone of voice. She suggested for John to try and communicate with Sarah. He looked at the little old lady like she had just snapped. She said, you have to try John, you have to do something and that's the only thing I can think of. John then realized that she was right and thought it just might work. As long as Charlotte was a part of Sarah, maybe she'd be able to talk to him. John nodded to Mrs. Darcy and waited for her reassurance. He slowly walked towards Sarah and knelt down on the floor in front of her. Cautiously, he reached out his hand to touch her and she quickly pulled away. Then their eyes met and John knew she was terrified of him. She didn't even want to look at him, so she covered her face with her hands. Mrs. Darcy saw what was happening. She walked over and sat in the rocking chair that was close to Sarah. She reached out and gently placed her hand on her shoulder as she said, My dear Sarah, the man is here to help you. He won't cause you any harm and if you ever want to find peace, open yourself to him. We're trying hard to find the truth. Can you help us? We want to help you and your Captain find your eternal peace. Sarah slowly responded to Mrs. Darcy's voice and dropped her hands away from her face. She opened her mouth to speak and the words came rolling out. She was startled by the sound that came from her lips.

She timidly looked at John and Mrs. Darcy and the fear in her eyes seemed to melt away. She said, You are truly here to help. John slowly reached out to touch her hand. He said, Yes we'll help you if we can, but we don't know what to do. Can you tell us how to find the whole truth? Please trust us? We really want to help. And now finally, with signs of great pain in her voice. Sarah begins to tell her tragic story....

*It's a very cold and rainy day in November. The day is the twenty second or twenty third. You see, I'm really not sure, because of the great sorrow I've been feeling. It seems that I've been in a daze since the news of Joe's death. I simply can't stand the pain, it hurts so badly. But then suddenly I realized I had to face the awful truth alone. "Suddenly she crumbled, she broke into heart wrenching sobs". Oh God! what will I do? Everyone will know the horrible truth. Now her memory flows back to the day it all began. She said, it's a very hot and muggy afternoon in August. I told mother I was going to the house to work in the gardens. I love the garden's and I felt so much pride in them. I never realized that I alone could make something so beautifully. They were perfect and I worked on them all the day and into the early evening hours. I realized it was getting late, for I lost all track of time. I gathered all my tools and put them away and headed for home. It would be dark before I got there if I didn't hurry.

So quickly I got back to the carriage and headed up the lane. Nearing the top, I looked over the knoll and saw a man in the shadows of a tree. He sat on his horse and watched as I continued out the lane. The man hit his horse and rode hard until he got to the lane just a few feet ahead of my carriage. I panicked, I cracked the whip and it came down hard. My horse lunged forward, my in tensions were to run him down. He laughed and as he did, he sounded as though he was the devil himself. His horse leaped forward and sideways making the path clear for me to pass. In my fear I whipped the poor animal pulling my carriage, unmercifully. He bound forward as fast as he could, but it was of no use. The man chased me down and jumped onto the carriage. He pulled the reins from me and I remembered he was much stronger than I. We struggled and fought until I had no more strength. He hit me and I fell back into the seat, then I realized we had turned and were headed back to the house. When he pulled up my horse he dragged me from the carriage. My dress caught on the seat and I fell to the ground. The man grabbed me by the hair and drug me to my feet. He was headed to the house and at this point, I fought like a wild cat. That was Joe's house and this trash would never go in there. Even if it cost me my life and it nearly did. Now, I only wish that I would of died that day. But, instead of dying I fainted from exhaustion.

When I finally came around the man was gone. My body hurt all over and I knew in an instant what had happened. The abdominal pain was severe and I felt blood oozing from between my thighs. I had just been raped, the bastard just stole my virginity. I tried to collect myself but it was hopeless. My clothing was torn and my under garments were completely gone. Then it accured to me. I have to gather myself and get home, Mother will be worried sick. As I got to the carriage it was most difficult boarding, but I managed and I drove the horses home to the point of exhaustion. When I got there I slipped into the house without my mother seeing me. I went straight in for a bath. The need to cleanse my body and soul was quite urgent, for I never wanted anyone to learn the filthy truth. This is something I had to deal with alone.

At this time Sarah sat quietly, she wept softly. The silence was unbearable. John and Mrs. Darcy sat quietly and waited to see what Sarah would do next. Soon Sarah began to weaken and the image of Charlotte came through. Mrs Darcy spoke softly and said to Charlotte. Charlotte don't fight her dear. She needs you to relax and let her come through again. Just relax everything will be fine, I promise, and as soon as she promised. Sarah returned and continued to tell her story.

She spoke softly as she said. I carried the burden of the truth alone and kept my dirty secrets. I prayed for Joe to come home, I had the need to tell him. No matter what the cost, but I couldn't do it in a letter and I prayed every day, that God would take this disgusting feeling away. It was hard dealing with my burden, but I lived from day to day. Then when I thought things would be getting better, they got worse. I realized that over a month has gone by and I haven't received my monthly. Immediately I knew that deep inside of me was growing a child to that awful man..... Silence filled the room as Sarah hung her head. She rolled herself up into a little ball and wept softly. She looks like a small child who was living in total terror. And suddenly she straighten right up and began to tell her story from where she left off... About three months have gone by and on this day I didn't have the courage to get out of bed, but somehow I managed. Then I received word of Joe's death and my whole world collapsed. I loved him so, and I knew I couldn't go on without him. The emptiness and the pain was more than I could bare and right then and there I decided to take my life. I planned it all out, but when it came right down to it I found that I was a coward. I didn't have the courage to go through with it. But that day wasn't a total loss. God answered my prayers; Later in the day I was feeling cramps in my lower belly. I was at the house when it all happened. Soon the pain became unbearable and I finally realized what was happening. I was all alone but that made things better for me. Now, I can surely hide the truth. After a long and very painful ordeal, it was finally over. I was extremely weak but I managed to drag myself out of bed. The bed clothing was a bloody mess.

I looked closely at the little form that laid in the middle of the mess. At this point my emotions were very mixed. Then, I rolled all the linens in to a ball and in them contained the tiny fetus of the child I was carrying. I weakly staggered to the stairs and hung on to the railings as I carried the bundle down the steps. I had to make it to the outside to get rid of everything. When I got to the entrance door I had to hang on to the door to keep from falling on my face. I was so weak I thought I would black out but I managed to keep alert somehow. I wanted to bury everything as far away as possible, but I'm feeling to weak. I can't make it, I'll have to bury it in the rose garden. I got to the well and couldn't make it any further. My knees were extremely weak and I fell to the ground. From here I crawled out to the end of the garden and dug a shallow grave for the baby. I place the bundle in, but the hole wasn't big enough, so I had to dig more. This time I buried all of the filth and guilt that I have felt for the past three months and no one will ever know. And, as soon as I'm feeling stronger I'll dig it up and rebury it far, far away from here. But that day never came and the horrible truth is still buried out there in the rose garden....... At this point Sarah is growing weak. She straining to speak and beginning to fade. She fades in and out and then all of a sudden Charlotte begins to come through. Soon Sarah is gone and Charlotte collapsed on the floor. John knew instantly that Sarah was gone and couldn't help thinking, maybe for good.

Charlotte moaned as she opened her eyes. She knew that Sarah was there and was feeling great sadness as she said, do you think it'll be over now? "John was surprised with her question". He said to her. Do you remember what happened? Charlotte said, Yes! I remember everything. It was like I lived it for her once again and it almost drained me completely to tell her story. John helped Charlotte to her feet and got her to the sofa where she could regain some of her strength. She rested awhile and as she recovered they talked about the story Sarah had told them. They realized that out in the garden was the whole truth and possibly the reason why the spirits are so restless. They had to do something. The next thing John knew. Charlotte was on her feet and headed outside. They followed her to see what she was up to. She went straight to the tool shed and got a shovel for her and John. She came back out and handed one of the shovels to John and said we're going to dig even if it takes all night. We have to find what's out there. They headed to the rose garden opposite the one where Sarah was buried. If they found nothing there then they would dig up the other one. They dug until almost dark and the garden was a total shambles. The rose bushes that once stood there proudly and beautifully were now lying on the ground on the outer edge's of the garden.

The two were exhausted as Mrs. Darcy sat and watched in anticipation. Finally John threw down his shovel and got down on his hands and knees to dig with his hands. He said, I'm not sure but I think I may have found something. Charlotte ran to John and stood over him as he dug. Finally he pulled something from the soil. He held it in his hands and rubbed some of the dirt away. "He was stunned". There he stood holding the tiny skull of the baby that Sarah buried so many years ago. The skull was the size of a golf ball and very soft. John had to be very careful with it. He was afraid it would deteriorate in the fresh air. He reached in to his pocket and pulled his handkerchief out and wrapped the tiny skull in it to protect it. He then continued to dig to find more of the remains. After digging he found nothing more and found himself wondering what to do next. Mrs. Darcy sat quietly and watched as John tried to figure the right thing to do. She said to him.

John take the skull up the lane and bury it on the other side of the road. John was appalled by her statement. He said, why? This is the remains of Sarah's baby and it wouldn't be right to bury it somewhere else. Mrs. Darcy said, Yes what you say is true, but remember Sarah said she was going to bury it somewhere far away. So, it seems to me that you might be holding the evil of the rose garden, and until it's removed Sarah will remain restless. John thought about what Mrs. Darcy had said. He figured she was older and wiser than he, and decided to do exactly as she said to do. He walked up to the end of the lane and crossed over the main road to the other side. The property belonged to the neighbors, so he had to be quick. He didn't want anyone to see him and ask questions. He knelt down to open a hole large enough and deep enough for the little ball and when he finished burying it. He prayed for God to grant peace to the tiny little soul. As he walked away he felt like he had done a tremendous deed. He felt good and had no idea why. By the time John got back to the garden it was almost dark. Charlotte and Mrs. Darcy sat at the well and waited for his return. They were talking about the life of Sarah and the horrible truth that died with her. John helped Mrs. Darcy to the house and they all had a feeling of peace come over them. By this time Charlotte was exhausted, so John and Mrs. Darcy fixed something to eat. With everything that happened they didn't have any supper. When the meal was ready they ate and recapped all the happenings of the day. John reminded the women that the Tomb would be opened once again in the morning, and Sarah would be put in her final resting place. As he spoke he got up from the table and went to the window. He stood and looked out into the night and there again right before his eyes appeared the Wall of Energy.

One thing that John noticed right away was the greenish blue haze wasn't quite as dense as before, and then the music began to play. He turned to tell the women to come and look, when he saw in the doorway the apparition of Sarah. He pointed and the women looked in that direction. Sarah, by this time was moving slowly towards Charlotte. As Sarah got closer, Charlotte stood up and Sarah emerged right into Charlotte's body.

John felt extreme panic as he witnessed the transformation. Charlotte was gone and Sarah is now standing in her place. But this time somehow things are different. Sarah smiled at John and Mrs. Darcy. She had a strange look on her face, almost as though she was happy. As she smiled she floated across the floor and went through the door. John grabbed Mrs. Darcy by the arm and they followed Sarah. She floated through the hall to the front door. As she approached the door it swung open and Sarah disappeared through it into the night. She continued across the porch and down the steps and as she got to the bottom she followed the walkway towards the cemetery. John stood and stared as Sarah approached the energy. He was filled with mixed emotions. He felt sympathy for Sarah, yet he feared for Charlotte's life. He felt that she was in great danger, but didn't dare interfere. He was helpless as he watched what was about to happen.

Finally his emotions took over, he began to go after Sarah when Mrs. Darcy reached out and grabbed him by the arm. She looked up at him and said, No John you mustn't interfere. You know it will only endanger Charlotte more. John knew she was right and stood and watched with terror in his eyes. The energy was still strong and possibly to strong for the human form. But Sarah still moved slowly towards it. John and Mrs. Darcy followed at a safe distance. John felt the great need to be as near to Charlotte as possible and Mrs.

Darcy stayed right by his side. They stopped as Sarah did and looked out through the energy. There just on the other side appeared the apparition of the Captain. He extended his arms towards Sarah and right behind him in the back ground stood Jessie. John thought, That's strange, I haven't seen the little old man in some time. Why is he showing himself now? But John didn't have much time to think about Jessie. Sarah was on the move again and headed into the wall of energy. As she entered into the waves of current, fireballs flew every-where. Then came a chain of explosions, sparks flew into the sky like thousands of fireworks that had gone off at one time. And suddenly Sarah walked right into the wall of fire and smoke. John screamed for Charlotte as Sarah entered into the burning inferno and he knew in his heart that he would never see Charlotte again.

As Sarah disappeared into the fire the music began to play louder and louder. After it reached an ear piercing tone the wall of energy began to disintegrate, bolts of energy shot up into the heavens and then the wall of energy faded completely out of sight. It's finally been destroyed.

As John stood by helplessly he was in a state of shock. He stood by and watched Charlotte walk right into the fire and didn't lift a finger to help her. His mind was dazed as he stood there frozen to the ground. His heart was heavy, for he knew down deep inside that he has lost Charlotte forever. His eyes were filled with blinding tears as he looked out across the cemetery. Sarah was now in the arms of the Captain and as they embraced the music began to play louder and louder. The apparition of the Captain moved away from Sarah to arms length. He began to sway to the music and soon they were dancing to Sarah's favorite melody. The Sweetheart's Waltz. They danced and danced until finally the sky opened right up and the Heavens invited their spirits in. But they didn't go, for some reason they stayed. At that point in time, there came a peace all over the land. The mist and heavy haze has disappeared and the sky rolled with heavy black clouds. It was pitch black, you couldn't see your hand in front of your face. John spun around to see if Mrs. Darcy was okay, he spoke to her and she answered and said, I'm fine, but look out into the cemetery. What is that? John turned around and looked.

He saw a very dim glow in the middle of the cemetery. In just seconds the glow became brighter and then the little old man appeared in the middle of the warm light.

In a surprised tone Mrs. Darcy said, Well I'll be, It's Jessie and he's trying to say something. But they couldn't understand what he was saying. Finally Jessie motioned for them to come to him. John did exactly as Jessie wanted, he figured he has already lost Charlotte and had nothing more to lose. He carefully walked slowly towards the old man. He was almost to Jessie, when he stumbled and fell. He was trying to get back to his feet when he touched something warm next to him. He looked up and Jessie was moving towards him. The glow that was hovering around him was lighting up the ground. Soon Jessie was close enough for John to see Charlotte laying beside him. She was turning blue and John knew instantly that she was dead... John dropped back to his knees and wept over her lifeless body. In his grief he questioned the Lord, and in his sorrow he lost control. The person he loved more than life itself was gone and he said, God how could you do this to us? What did we do to deserve this? Why are you punishing me? John then laid his body across the body of his wife and cried as his heart was breaking. When John came to realize that his wife was dead. He thought he would carry her to the house. He didn't want her to lay on the cold wet ground. He put his arm under her neck and the other under her thighs and started to lift her when he heard something. He stopped and stood perfectly still. He waited to see what it was that made the sound.

He hard it again only louder this time. It was a moan of some kind and he listened quietly. Then suddenly Charlotte began to move and she moaned again. John was spell bound, He stared at his wife without saying a word. He watched as Charlotte opened her eyes and broke down crying. Charlotte grabbed him and held him tight, she said, Honey, don't cry. It's all over and she knew that Sarah and Joe have found their peace. John picked Charlotte up from the ground, and as he held her he turned to Jessie and said, I'll be forever grateful for what you've done. Jessie looked at him and said, It was my pleasure sir, and instantly vanished into the darkness. John stood Charlotte on her feet and they stood and looked out into the darkness. They watched as the clouds cleared and the sky was beautiful once again. Out in the cemetery, a ray of light descended out of the heavens and warmly lighted the figures in it's path. The Captain and his beloved Sarah were still waltzing to the melody and Jessie stood by at a distance and watched them in all their enchantment. He was a faithful soul. He stayed on earth to help free the desperate spirits. Without him they would have been lost forever. He too, deserves to rest and his reward will be eternal peace. Then finally after one hundred and thirty years. There came a peace that was very well deserved. The truth has been found and the evil has been removed. The child has been reburied and the tiny soul has been freed.

Now Sarah and her beloved Captain danced and danced until the Heavens finally opened to invite them in. Warm rays of heavenly light shown down on them as they drifted up and towards the sky and soon they would be entering into the hereafter to be at peace to their blankets and the picnic basket and headed down the road. They were both excited. They felt like they were going on an adventure. They drove for a mile or so when on the right hand side of the road came an opening in the weeds. Charlotte said to John turn here. John said, turn where? There's no where to turn. Charlotte said, that's nonsense I turned right here when the kids and I were here. There's a road in those weeds. He said okay, I hope your right and made the turn to go into the lane. As the car enter the old lane the weeds seemed to magically open to make room for the car. Then John could see his way clear to the top of the lane. As they slowly topped the knoll they looked ahead and down the lane there it stood. The old house and just as Charlotte described it. John was amazed with the sight. He looked at Charlotte and said, By God your right there is a house down there. But look at it, it's completely covered with trees and ivy. The roof was impossible to see. Charlotte said, I'm so excited I want to see more. We can walk down from here. John was a little reluctant. He said we're probably trespassing already. Charlotte said, Oh bull there doesn't look like there's been any one around here for years. John looked at Charlotte with a gleam in his eyes and said, let's do it. The adventurer has finally taken over as he said, but we have to be real careful. There are probably a lot of snakes in the high weeds and brush that we can't see. They took the children by the hands and started down the lane.

The weeds and briers were thick, they clung to their clothing and dug into their flesh until they bled. John tried to fight his way through to make a path but it was of no use. Finally he said to Charlotte. You stand right there and I'll be right back. He went to the car to find something to cut down the brush. The only thing in the trunk was a tire iron and he thought, this will have to do. He went back to where he left Charlotte standing and said, my tire iron will save the day and it did. It wouldn't cut but it did beat a path big enough for them to pass through. John swung the iron and soon he was successful at making a path. It was a small narrow path but enough that they could go through without being all chewed up. Soon they were close enough to give the house a better look. He continued down the lane and soon he came to an old well. It was completely covered with weeds and as he pulled the brush he was amazed to find it in beautiful condition. He said to Charlotte, look all the stones are in their original position. The only thing wrong with it is the roof is a little rotted but besides that it was perfect. John continued to beat down the weeds and finally he had a Hugh circle cleared around the well. In the circle stood two stone benches, one on each side of the well. He said, they must have been beautiful in their day. Now John too, is excited. Now he wants to get a closer look at the house.

Printed in the USA
CPSIA information can be obtained
at www.ICGtesting.com
LVHW071950170923
758232LV00084B/746